R. Wilberforce Starr

The people's life of the Rev. Peter MacKenzie: the man and his work by

the Rev. Wilberforce Starr

R. Wilberforce Starr

The people's life of the Rev. Peter MacKenzie: the man and his work by the Rev. Wilberforce Starr

ISBN/EAN: 9783743377042

Manufactured in Europe, USA, Canada, Australia, Japa

Cover: Foto ©Raphael Reischuk / pixelio.de

Manufactured and distributed by brebook publishing software (www.brebook.com)

R. Wilberforce Starr

The people's life of the Rev. Peter MacKenzie: the man and his work by

the Rev. Wilberforce Starr

THE PEOPLE'S LIFE

OF THE

Rev. PETER MACKENZIE:

THE MAN AND HIS WORK.

BY THE

REV. R. WILBERFORCE STARR.

———

LONDON:
W. H. SMITH & SON, 186, STRAND, W.C.
TAYLOR'S, 26 and 27, HIGH HOLBORN, W.C.
LEEDS:
Printed and Published by HARRISON & WAIDE, KIRKSTALL ROAD.

——

1896.

INDEX.

" Hush ! I will give you this leaf to keep.
    See, I shut it inside the sweet cold hand !
There, that is our secret, go to sleep !
    You will wake and remember and understand."

INTRODUCTION.

Methodists of all denominations, and hundreds of thousands of others who are of sister Churches, and even more still who belong to no Church at all, can scarcely yet credit that the great-hearted and wondrously-gifted Peter Mackenzie is no longer in their midst. His cheery voice and sunny smile at the cab-stand or ticket-office, on the domestic doorstep, or public platform, will be heard and seen no more; and the multitudes who hung upon his lips with delight and profit must look now for another instructor, or remain ungathered. His wise and witty words yet linger in hundreds of towns and villages, and will be tenderly repeated with thankful acknowledgment for many a long year to come. The places that knew him shall know him no more, and no other can fill them. He had no forerunner, and he can have no successor. The record of such a man will be safe and sacred in the hands of his Church, and indeed far beyond, while every item concerning his work and life will be treasured up with more than miserly care.

Already the Life of this wonderful man has been written with discrimination, though with necessary haste, and several attempts have been made, with more or less accuracy and taste, to give the eager multitude a cheap popular account of the man beloved and known so well.

From exceptional opportunities of personal knowledge and intercourse extending over long years, I have, with reverent love, set down here the result of that knowledge with associated information from only reliable quarters. Concerning such a man, rumour has been busy for years, and will continue to find unenviable occupation. All kinds of absurd and impossible things have been and will be connected with his name and work. Leading a momentary, fugitive life, the northern papers have been full of them. Sifting the wheat from the chaff, I have here endeavoured to present the man as he really was, and his work as it was splendidly done, hoping that the attempt of one who loved and revered him will find acceptance and acknowledgment in not a few hearts.   R. W. S.

REV. PETER MACKENZIE.

CHAPTER I.

LIFE IN SCOTLAND.

IN a mere scrap of a diary the subject of this small book records the fact of his birth thus :—

"I was born in Glen Shee, North Highlands of Scotland, on the 11th of November, 1824."

That is all we have of the child's start in life; and are left in almost total darkness concerning the antecedents of his family. How Peter's father, an Englishman, came so far north we know not, but thus it was his famous boy was born under the shadow of the Perthshire hills.

Glen Shee, a small Scotch village, is quite out of the run of the tripper and tourist, and even the wandering easel or camera; but, like many an obscure hamlet, it has leaped into sudden fame as being the quiet nook where a man, whose unblemished name will long be cherished as a "household word," first saw the light.

Born in a country famous for its "brown heath and shaggy wood; land of the mountain and the flood;" its tumbling seas round its broken coast-line; its majestic mountains and lordly forests and fertile 'straths;' it would be difficult to say how much of the scenes of his childhood followed and clung to him, and, moreover, gave unconscious colour and inspiration to his developing genius and its amazing triumphs.

Too young for the charge of any dominie, we can readily picture the toddling bairn as he wandered by the rocky burn, paddling in its clear sweet waters, or eagerly watching the spotted trout his little hands longed to possess. We fancy him now and then lost among the heathery hills as he was tempted to follow the song of the mavis, or the cry of the grouse. Tied down by incessant labour in dismal villages and congested towns in after years, his heart and thought often went back in happy recalling to the days of his childhood at peaceful Glen Shee.

Though born in Scotland, where he passed nearly twenty years of his life, there was, however, always more about him of the Northumbrian than the Scot. Indeed, his after methods of speech and gesture often raised the question as to whether the Liffey or the Tyne could not have put in a very presentable claim to his possession. He might have hailed from either river-bank, and have been an additional honour to any neighbourhood.

As the manner of some Scotchmen is, he seldom revisited the scenes of his childhood, and the accepted invitations to the "land o' cakes" were not numerous. Though he loved the Scotch people, and was not by any means unfamiliar with their best writers. I have seldom heard him quote any of his great countrymen; but when he did give a bit of Burns, with whose genius he had not a little in common, it was with a smack the renowned Ayrshire ploughman would have relished.

But those early days of childhood, undoubtedly, helped to make and mould the man; and, when in after days he took his crowded congregations by storm, and held possession of his astonished audiences, the triumphant speaker was in no small measure indebted to the undying memories of his young Highland life, and its romantic associations.

Little is known of his parents. The father was no " Belted Knight," or,

" Tenth transmitter of a foolish face,"

as poor slashing Churchill puts it; being only a small cottar-farmer, looking after some few acres, upon which he raised his crops, and tended his little flock of sheep.

It seems as if Peter was to be a traveller from the beginning; as owing to dire exigencies his father found it necessary to "move on;" and the little fellow had to say "good bye" to the dear old glen of his childhood. And when, after long years of exhausting toil, he "sat down," as the curious Methodist phrase has it, he often said playfully, " I never ran about so much ! "

The family left Perthshire when the child was hardly four years of age, and the strong man would relate, as he recalled the incident with infinite merriment, the story of his being somehow lost in the streets of Dundee, where he was " run in " by friendly " Bobbies."

At Commerton Links, in Fifeshire, Mackenzie's father started life anew, and the so-called education of the boy was commenced. How much of the three R's he got we cannot imagine, in any case it was not manifest in his mysterious hand-writing, the scraps of which, however, are almost sacredly cherished by thankful friends to-day all over the country. But the boy could use his inquisitive eyes and ears to purpose. "The boy is father to the man," and to the last Peter was ever on the alert for anything that would illustrate his message, or succeed his mission.

On the settlement of Mackenzie's father at Mildway, between Logie and the dull, quaint little town of Cupar Fife, the sturdy boy found employment on a small farm, at what must have been to him, at his age, a royal income —ten shillings a week! But he obtained something else, whose value cannot be found in the vocabulary of mammon. Here he came in touch with family prayer, and, as he says, "his first good impressions."

In this year of Burn's centenary, one cannot but at once recall—perhaps the very best thing the marvellous ploughman ever did—"The Cottar's Saturday Night." Burns knew the failings and hypocrisies of the "unco' guid," but he also knew the worth and wealth to his country of people like David Longley, men who have unconsciously made or strengthened the moral backbone of Scotland, and made it more than famous for the greatest thinkers and speakers in the interests of truth and righteousness the world has ever known. Surely Burns had in his subtle brain picturesqueness, that lone farm house in the great "strath," when he wrote:—

> "The cheerfu' supper done, wi' serious face,
> They round the ingle form a circle wide;
> The sire turns o'er, wi' patriarchal grace.
> The big ha' Bible, ance his father's pride:

His bonnet reverently is laid aside,
　　His lyart haffets wearing thin and bare ;
Those strains that once did sweet in Zion glide,
　　He wails a portion with judicious care,
　　And, ' let us worship God ! ' he says, with solemn air."

Following the growing, and often hungry lad, we find
him spending two years of comparative comfortlessness at
Logie, hard by Cupar, where the only incident that broke
the miserable monotony was the jogging to the market
town once a week. These were weekly holidays indeed!
There are stories of the old farm house on fire—Peter
would be on the scene you may be sure;—of his experience
with bad-tempered horses, and, judging from his quiet
hints, bad-tempered men; but the brave, sturdy lad held
on, and, after hiring himself at St. James' Market, Cupar
Fife, to David Arnot, Wester Colsel, near Auchermuchty,
stayed over three years in the new service.

Think of it! Peter Mackenzie standing in the market
place—*any* market place—and mentally or audibly saying,
" No man hath hired me ! "

When the Great Master called His servant into a
wider employ, a few years hence, the clamorous demands
for his services fairly bewildered the herd-laddie of the
Perthshire hills.

How Peter could have managed to have saved five
pounds out of the thirteen he received, during the three
years' hard labour, I cannot conceive! Of course the
natural grace, gift, or whatever else it may be, of thrift, may
account for much; but the wonderful, or, as some said,
eccentric generosity, displayed by the future minister,
makes it a marvel how he could have held so much wealth
in possession so long.

There is no record during these years of anything that would suggest indications of prominence on either side of the Alps of intellect or morals. It was a time of dull, hard work, and, strong as he was, wearisome toil. So the stalwart youth grew into the young man, and we find him in the stirring town of Dundee, where he spent two years. His country eyes were opened there somewhat, for he says, "I saw much of town life, but did not see much good."

He often brought Jehu into his sermons and lectures, but few knew that he himself was hailed before the Dundee bailies on a charge of furious driving, or aiding and abetting a brother whip. But so it was. There is no record of the solemn tribunal that I can find. Peter was always fond of a horse or a donkey—his early love—that could "go." Said he, in after years, to a noted minister's wife whom he was driving from Newcastle to Gateshead, and who expressed fears as her friend cut ugly corners in a somewhat perilous fashion, "I'll take you like eggs," which the enthusiastic driver did, and he brought the lady to her destination, much to her satisfaction.

Drifting from hamlet to town, the young man was maturing. With a singularly observant eye, he obtained stores of knowledge concerning nature and human nature, which readily came to his hand in after years, surprising his various audiences with the variety and correctness of his keen analyses, and picturesque, descriptive and dramatic power.

Peter must have been a brawny young fellow, getting on to his twentieth year, when in Dundee, where he lived for two years—very important years for him or any young man at his time of life. But little is known of that Dundee life.

These scanty items are all that we have of the early years of Peter, whose name is now only a precious memory. He was the last man to despise the homeliness of early surroundings, but whether in public or private, he seldom made reference—extended or minute—to the days of his young childhood and early manhood in the "auld countrie." But the days were not without their uses, and memories of their hard experiences were twisted into many a great public effort.

CHAPTER II.

———

IT is not to be wondered at that the strongly-built young man should begin to grow restless. He has left us no indication of his purposes and hopes at that time, but doubtless his life in Dundee broadened his outlook greatly, and gave him a growing longing to see more of the stirring world.

So the future Methodist orator—the "miners' darling," as he was to be—came south on tramp with three other adventurers, their object and hope being the coal pits of the Tyne or Wear. It is a far cry from the quiet farm-steads of Fifeshire to the dismal pit villages of the dusky coal-miners, where tens of thousands of men pursue their unwholesome and dangerous occupation among the sunless coal measures. Hogarth has given us a graphic description of the inimitable pic-nic to the Isle of Sheppy (surely these were the first Pickwickians), but it would require another Hogarth to paint the strange quartet. while on the road to Durham County! Mackenzie's companions are unknown, but we may be sure he "kept them alive;" however, in due course the wanderers found rest to the "sole of their foot," at Oxclose, near Washington, and speedily obtained new, if not congenial, employment in the pits. It must have been a strange new world indeed to Peter!

The coal miner! How few know anything of his toil, privation, and danger? Think of him, then, crouched in painful forms, half naked, in rugged, gloomy galleries where it is impossible to stand upright, with his tiny lamp, picking away in loneliness at the black treacherous mass. Now and then the sound of the "hurrier's" voice is heard— a welcome break in the awful monotony—but the usual noises that disturb the dreadful stillness are the gurgling, or splashing of dripping waters; the echoes occasioned by a distant fall of exploded coal, or the significant passing rush of escaped deadly gas. To the eyes of the uninitiated, the coal-miner, on stepping out of the "cage" after his six hours' spell, would present an almost inhuman aspect. Seemingly from another world he looks in his coarse flannels and rough attire, with blackened or grimed face as if he had no relations with the race above ground. But in hundreds of instances that forbidding object may in an hour or two be seen transformed, and even glorified, in the chair of a Methodist class meeting, or, maybe, standing up in the sacred desk itself, declaring with astonishing vehemence and accuracy the good news of God. Methodism won its first triumphs among the miners of Kingswood and the Tyne, and holds a premier place in their ranks and affections to-day; while not a few of her best sons in the ministry fought hard in the pit before they came to stand in the pulpit.

The unskilled labour of Peter was first employed in what was, years ago, about the poorest and hardest labour in the miné. A lad was required to serve the hewers with empty tubs, and remove them when filled, and such was Mackenzie's labour on the little winding dark tram roads of the pit at Oxclose, where he spent twelve months. What his thoughts were during that first year of underground life among the roughest of men and boys, we know not, but he obtained a treasured experience which, in after years, enabled him to touch a collier's life and work with such sympathetic power as to draw forth, on one occasion, the startling encomium, "He's a regular brick!" Could a D.D. of Oxford hope for a better plaudit, though expressed in the choicest Attic Greek?

This year's work must have developed the muscles, if not the mind and morals, of the coming man. Then Peter came to Haswell. It was a great change, but there were changes in store he little knew of.

The typical colliery village, with the usual one long straggling street of cheap, unsavoury dwellings, and a limited sprinkling of small chandlers and provision shops, was no very inviting place for work or rest. Everything was poor, mean, and unsightly. Coarseness was in evidence everywhere, even in the religion of the place, what little there was. But the new comer brought at least additional liveliness into it, and he was speedily recognised as a welcome toiler to the hive of pit men on account of his life and drollery, as he had been at Oxclose. "A canny sort of a chap," he could lead, and often did, the rough revels on the waste bits of ground, and even then showed himself a leader of men.

To those who remember his over-flowing life on the platform, it will be no strange news that he was excessively fond of tripping it on the village green, or indeed, anywhere. But though his deep guttural voice was far from musical, he was greatly in love with his fiddle, with whose strains he frequently edified or annoyed his neighbours. No wonder the strapping young fellow was in request far and wide, and few holidays could be considered complete without him.

CHAPTER III.

———

ETHODISM has created and started off on their travels many gifted and wondrously successful lay evangelists, who, though at times eccentric and revolutionary in their methods, have reaped large harvests, especially in poorly-cared-for districts. Such names as Billy Dawson, Sammy Hick, Billy Bray, Edward Brooke, Charles Richardson, Isaac Marsden, and scores of others at once suggest themselves.

Henry Reed, of Harrogate—Squire Reed, as he was known in his later years—was a remarkable man. He had his own rigid views of men and things, as well as his own hymn book, and not unfrequently tormented his guests at his grand Harrogate residence with pet religious whims and oddities. His givings were large, when a man could handle him, as the late Alexander McAulay knew to his joy when laying the foundations of the great Wesleyan Extensions in East London.

In one of his wandering excursions, Squire Reed turned up at the colliery village of Haswell. There is no account of the revivalist's visit left, save one, which deals with the conversion and transformation of Peter Mackenzie, and *that*, surely, was enough reward for a whole life of labour.

Urged by the persistent invitations of two fellow colliers, Mackenzie promised to attend an evening service, and did. There is no record of the sermon, but at its close there was an unusual excitement in the prayer meeting which followed. There were great stirrings in the depths of the young miner's heart, and, as Mr. Dawson says, "the good sowing of past days in the farmer's kitchen, at Mildean, and of the Bible readings at his own fireside, began to germinate."

Swayed with uncontrollable emotion, Peter stood up, and went forward to the "penitent form," as it used to be called. The Methodists have invented or adopted a more select and genteel method now, and the result is the Inquiry Room. But there was an unearthly grip on the man, and, as he knelt on the hard floor of the village chapel, the sweet words of an undying hymn calmed his soul's restlessness, and brought him comfort and strength that sustained him to the end. Here it is. Maybe eyes that have long neglected it, or that perchance have never seen it, may now realise its sweetness and gentle leading to the one and only refuge of soul satisfaction and peace. It cannot be printed too often.

> Rock of ages, cleft for me,
> Let me hide myself in Thee;
> Let the water and the blood,
> From Thy wounded side which flowed,
> Be of sin the double cure,
> Save from wrath and make me pure.

However important and successful the methods of modern Methodism may be when dealing with awakened and conscience-stricken men, arrested by the power of the Holy Ghost, there can be no question that the penitent form in years gone by was the place of spiritual crisis and salvation to hundreds of thousands of troubled souls. The mere act of going forth in the congregation meant, helped, and emphasised decision. Multitudes of saved men and women look back with thankful joy to the hour of pardon and peace, when, encouraged by the scrap of some tenderly apposite hymn, or gently whispered promise of big worth, or maybe in the midst of apparently unintelligent excitement, they caught sight of the great crimson cross, and found their long-sought rest. Whatever additions the complicated machinery of the Methodist Church requires and makes, it will be a matter for profoundest regret, as it will be a thing of unspeakable loss, if this help to Calvary is discarded.

There was no mistake about Peter Mackenzie's conversion, as one who was an onlooker says, "It was *instantaneous* and thorough." And why not instantaneous? The Lord's arm is not shortened, and he can cut short the work in righteousness, and bring to the climax of seemingly sudden victory unknown secret forces of spiritual impression, that openly culminate in the submission and salvation of possibly the most hopeless case.

"The wind bloweth where it listeth, thou canst not tell whence it cometh or whither it goeth; so is everyone that is born of the Spirit." The workings of that Spirit are various and manifold. The same Bible leaf that records the conversion of Lydia, "Whose heart the Lord *gently* opened," narrates the sudden and surprising salvation of the jailor of Philippi, who, with an earthquake about him, and a corresponding upheaval within him, was captured in the presence of his captives, and added to the strength of the early brotherhood of Christ. This side of hell, the Church has no right to give anybody up.

With a new world around him, because of a new heart within him, the young convert breasted the difficulties of the altered condition of things, not that he suffered persecution; he was too strong a man to play with, the whole colliery knew that; but the old allurements were many, subtle, and strong.

"Cease to do evil; learn to do well," is the emphatic and uncompromising command. But the mere force of habit often betrays and upsets men of Peter's class, and indeed, all beginners in the unaccustomed life. The spirit is willing, but the flesh is weak. The great difficulty, however, often is—to coin a word—to *unlearn*.

In this connection take the case of a Humber Keel-man, who, with scores of others of his order, was saved in the most out-and-out fashion. Speaking one night in the George Yard Band-meeting, with demonstrative satisfaction, he exclaimed, "Glory be to God, I'm getting on, I've only sworn twenty times this week!" No doubt for an ordinary average man, with anything pretending to even common decency, that number of "swears" would be more than sufficient for a lifetime, but when it is remembered that the man's vocabulary was largely made up of foul, though meaningless, expressions, and which gave colour and emphasis to also every other sentence, it must be conceded that the new convert was after all making rapid and splendid headway.

But the promised and sufficient grace of Heaven saved Peter in the strange new environment in which he found himself. He found the great saving secret, that He who is able to drive out of the human heart all forces of evil, can keep them out; that He who is able to save, is, and only He, able to keep; a blessed, comforting truth he was never tired of enforcing and illustrating down to the end of his days.

So Peter Mackenzie held on his way. Quoting from one who knew him intimately, Mr. Dawson narrates how, twelve months after the young miner's memorable conversion, he tramped from Haswell to Durham, with some of his companions, to hear his old friend Squire Reed. Referring to the gracious revival at Haswell, Mr. Reed spoke of a good Scottish brother who had been brought to Christ—a very promising case of conversion—" I wonder where he is now; whether he has held on his way?" asked the preacher. There was an immediate and startling rejoinder from the gallery: " I am here, Mr. Reed; praise the Lord, I am here ! " Yes, praise the Lord, he held on, and lived to hear the same sweet assuring testimony from many hundreds of men and women saved through his own ministry.

True, the young convert took some time—and what wonder?—in " rooting and grounding," while the watchful anxiety of his friends surrounded him with every sort of saving help, but he was " a tree of the Lord's right-hand planting," and speedily manifested an unexpected spiritual vigour and health, which promised and produced early fruitfulness.

Old things passed away. The Bible, never utterly
disused, became his constant companion, and the
Wesleyan hymn-book his cherished manual of song;
while the Chapel and class-room now met all the moods
and needs of his exciting nature. A marvellous deliverance from a tragic death in the pit no doubt helped to
strengthen and harden his religious impressions, but
having " put his hand to the plough," he looked not back,
and became more ready and eager for his Master's service
day by day.

For long years Peter Mackenzie went in and out
among "all sorts and conditions of men," as old Dr.
Johnson liked to phrase it, and seemed to know them and
their environment in a wonderfully minute way; but his
practical and sympathetic knowledge of miners and pits
clung to him all through his romantic public course, and
no dizzy height of popularity made him forget the " hole
of the pit," and his old uncouth, but kindly, associates.

There were coarse people in the village of every kind,
and in not a few instances brutality was resorted to, with
the usual following interview with the magistrates.
Peter's noble sense of chivalry was more than once
appealed to, when he saw, as he often did, weary women
struck down by drink-sodden men, and there are stories
yet lingering at Haswell which show the young miner's
courage and high sense of honour in a wonderful light.
Regarding one lively incident, where he rescued a forlorn
woman from the clutches of her maddened husband, he
would say in after years as the memory of the tussle came
back to him, " aye, but I dusted his jacket, right l." And
the curious merry brightness of the preacher's eyes left no

need for any violent exercise of the imagination. In after years the wife-beater and his brawny assailant were found strangely associated, and the former in his poverty only knew what the extent of the generosity of the latter was.

In not a few of his lectures Peter expatiated on the women of Bible story. Who can forget, those who heard him, his inimitable description of such characters as Rachel, "Mrs. Potiphar," "Mrs. Job," Ruth, Jezebel, Delilah, "Mrs. Boam"—as he called her for convenience— and his greatly beloved Queen Esther. "Bless her, I've had many a good talk with her; she has brought us hundreds of pounds." In these same lectures, and so in his sermons, there lurk an infinite variety of sly hits at man's weakness and woman's wit; but how was it to fare with himself? He had been away from Dundee nearly two years, and was beginning to grow tired of lodgings, as all sensitive young men must, and do.

Of course there are all sorts of stories about his court-ship, but it will be well to remember the grain of salt, and even the pinch of snuff. The end of it was that he married a daughter of one John Thompson, a small farmer; and Peter and his Mary started a new home of their own after a wisely extended courtship. It was a happy match, and, near on to the golden wedding anniversary, the kindred souls daily manifested loving communion and helpfulness. The house was poor enough,

> "But true love is at home in a cottage."

It is an old and oft-quoted saying, that "a man is what his wife makes him." With tender respect, be it noted, that the comparatively unknown wife of the great preacher was to the end his best counsellor and help, and

she was that from the first.   It may be that at the start of
married life their tastes and experiences ran much in the
same channel;   but from the beginning of Peter
Mackenzie's public course, it was noted, as a matter of
thankful surprise, how the good wife fell in with the
changed order of things.   Votes of grateful thanks were
showered upon the husband everywhere, but surely, the
Methodist public at least owe a respectful and hearty vote
of thanks to the wife and mother, who ungrudgingly under-
took the burden of her rising family and household cares,
in order that her husband might meet the growing claims
that were made upon his time and strength.   When wo
think of Peter in all the blaze of popular success and
public excitement, let us not forget the many and serious
sacrifices made by the mother of his children, for the good
of the Church they both loved so well.

It is not often that a publican appears in the character
of a librarian—the beer-stained newspaper being generally
the only literature on loan ; and in Peter's early days there
were no such immensely useful institutions as Free
Libraries in small towns and villages ; but from some
friendly John Barleycorn he obtained some stirring books
occasionally, which give suggestive evidence that all his
spare time was not spent on the bowling green, or when
dancing "toe and heel" to the strains of another's fiddle
or his own.

It is very pleasant and significant so to find the man,
who afterwards, and to the end, was such a voracious reader
among books.   Never addicted to the coarse, brutal vices
of his class, as we have it on the best testimony, we get
here a peep into the opening out of mental inquiry, which

could not be satisfied with mere athletic sport, or boisterous merriment. And very pleasant it is also to note the amazing advance which colliery districts and others of their kind have made since that day. In addition to the multiplied and regular religious services, the library, lecture, reading-room, and science classes, put within reach of the lowliest the opportunity of rising to higher and nobler things.

Peter Mackenzie's right hand thumb bore traces of injury which he carried to the grave, and at times he would expatiate on its cause with inimitable drollery. In common with his mates, he conceived an intense pleasure in donkey-driving or racing, and, astride the astonished animal, with his face to the quadruped's tail, Peter was in high glee and in a great state of satisfaction. One day, however, the two had some kind of difference, which resulted in the partial mutilation of the rider's thumb—the donkey having more vice than its owner. Peter had something to remind him of the tussle to the end of his days, and the "moke," he would say, with a merry twinkle in his eye, had cause to remember it too.

Mr. Dawson tells a story in this connection which is so good and characteristic of his hero, that we record it here.

"I remember him," says Mr. Dawson, "relating to me how he went once to Houghton-le-Spring, to enjoy what was called 'The Feast,' a species of rustic fair and merry-making held annually. He sported for the occasion a pair of white pantaloons; and what was his chagrin, on returning from the fair to the inn where he had stabled his donkey, to find saddle and bridle gone, and, as if that were not enough provocation, the perverse animal had rolled itself vigorously in the mire of the inn yard, and was not fit to lay a hand upon. White trousers and a mud-plastered donkey formed an incongruous combination, and the disgusted sportsman returned home with the conviction that the way of transgressors can not only be hard, but at times disagreeably soft.''

It is not a difficult matter to picture the young husband bravely toiling in the dark pits, and loyally standing by the sanctities of his humble home, while his overflowing life found courses of comparatively harmless merriment, though at times rough enough in every direction. Turned into another channel, his exuberant life became a surprisingly attractive power, and aided a moral force which was of incalculable benefit to unnumbered thousands.

CHAPTER IV.

REVIVAL WORK.

———

THE restless, excitable nature of Mackenzie made it imperative for him to be closely associated with all that was of life and movement among the people, through whose loving, sympathetic efforts he has gained his chiefest good. Like a bicycle rider, he was bound to go on, or go off. Only what was of an enthusiastic order could meet his need, and the church of his choice has met and provided for such undeveloped and untrained energies as his.

It is to be feared that too often the cultured, and more often the imaginary cultured, classes in the church, whose only ground of superiority frequently consists of a social standing, hold aloof from the seemingly unintelligent noise and stir of enthusiastic prayer meetings, band meetings, and "open-airs." Humanly speaking, whatever else saved him, only this order of things could have kept him. With the new life pulsing in his whole being, he needed and found everything that he required for its maintenance and development in that unpretentious Methodist Chapel, at Haswell.

Revivals of religion were common in Peter's hamlet and the pit villages for miles round. The peculiar and difficult life of the people, somehow, required an occasional spiritual "shake-up," and in their glowing excitements Peter found just what fed and broadened his own growing spiritual enthusiasm. He tramped for miles in order to get and give in the blessed work; and, not content with the services his own church afforded, we find him lending a generous hand wherever special services were held. Such meetings were to him not only a matter of religious temperament, but of spiritual life itself. In the thick of a rousing prayer meeting, he was seen and heard in all his glory; and, as we see him with strong, tender hand on the shoulder of some sobbing brother miner, speaking or shouting words of comfort and hope, he appears at his best; and though we follow him to far different scenes and methods of declaring the same gospel in after years, we see him to no greater advantage. His demonstrative gladness, and sharp unexpected outbursts of holy desire or approval will not soon be forgotten by tens of thousands; great numbers of whom will be in the crown of his endless rejoicings. "Glory!" "Praise the Lord!" "Hallelujah!" were expressions always on his tongue; and though repeated in what with many would suggest meaningless monotony, in his lips they had a freshness and a significance to his last hour.

A great favourite hymn of his was the one which has been sung with overwhelming emotion by Methodist congregations for the last hundred years:

"I'll praise my Maker while I've breath," &c.

Whether on the cab stand, or in the drawing-room, his happy soul found audible, though unexpected, opportunities for expression. But such were never mechanical—shall I say—and though they might occasionally startle, and even annoy religious sobriety, they were never regarded as mere religious "mouthings," but rather as the necessary escapement of the spiritual force of a nature which could only find vent and satisfaction in that form.

Peter went through, and saw something of the deplorable Methodist Reform movement, which touched even his village, though to no great extent. The two great parties concerned made many and terrible mistakes—it is easy to see it all now—but it is hoped that the healing touch of time and grace will speedily bring both together again, and that the dying feud will soon end in a generous clasping of hands. Of this there are glad and significant signs. The deep spiritual life of the society at Haswell, though often disturbed by somewhat fierce controversy, saved it and Peter. In the thick of the fight, no less a deputation than William Morley Punshon put in an appearance. It was at the Annual Missionary Meeting, and the coming man who was to be renowned throughout the whole Methodist world, was introduced to Peter Mackenzie! Both were climbing unconsciously the dangerous pyramid of popularity, though on opposite sides; and in the ending of the effort, left records of unapproached successes their church will never suffer to die out. Well may Mr. Dawson say, when referring to this incident: "At the close he shook hands with the impetuous miner, little dreaming that in a few years this unlettered working man would, as lecturer and preacher, win a fame as wide as his own."

The Sunday School has been, in hundreds of instances, a great "school of the prophets," and the early impetus and training of not a few illustrious ministers ought to be traced to that elementary, but all-important institution. But no rule or order could fit in with the young boisterous life of the eager "free lance," and this leads us on to the first scenes of his public ministration.

No doubt Peter had exhorted in a preliminary way at many a stirring gathering, but in no way had as yet received the usual official recognition and direction of his church. But an opportunity came all unexpectedly at last, and the young glowing exhorter stood up in the place of a good local brother, and, taking the narrative of Bartimeus, delivered an address of such extraordinary energy, point, and eloquence, that fairly astonished his congregation, and, while commanding tears and laughter by turn, carried all before it. It certainly was a remarkable effort, as Mr. Cuthbert testifies in a deeply interesting communication made through Mr. R. Garnett of Coxhoe, in the *North Eastern Daily Gazette.*

This is Mr. Cuthbert's account of Peter Mackenzie's first sermon, which cannot be read without curious and affectionate interest.

"It occurred to me," says Mr. Garnett, "that Mr. Cuthbert was one of the congregation who heard Mr. Mackenzie's first deliverance from the pulpit. I paid Mr. Cuthbert a visit, made known my business, and he very frankly tendered to me the following particulars: 'I think, Mr. Cuthbert, it was at Sherburn Hill, in the county of Durham, where Mr. Mackenzie made his first effort at preaching from the pulpit?' 'Yes, I distinctly remember

the time; it was in a building that was used both as
schoolroom and chapel.' 'Can you give any valid proof
that the time you refer to was Mr. Mackenzie's first effort
in the pulpit?' 'From his own statement at the time I
am satisfied of this. In his apology at the beginning of
his discourse he reminded his hearers that they were not
to expect much from him, as he had never been in a pulpit
before, not even to snuff the candles. It may be necessary
to explain that *moulds* or *dips* forty or fifty years ago
were an indispensable requisite in village chapels during
the long nights, and the snuffing very often had to be
done by the preacher himself in the pulpit. If the
manipulation was not very expertly performed and any
mishap took place, a general titter would pass through the
congregation at the preacher's expense.'

'Was there anything in the preacher or his discourse
that impressed you as being out of the ordinary?' 'I
remember his intense earnestness, humour, and witty
remarks, made an impression on my mind which I have
never forgotten.'

'Do you remember if this, his first effort in the pulpit,
was regarded by the congregation who heard him as a
success, or was it considered a failure?' 'It was certainly
regarded as a success, and much appreciated and talked
about for a long time afterwards.'

'Do you remember the subject of his discourse on the
occasion?' 'The subject, I think, was *Blind Bartimeus*,
but I cannot say positively.' 'Do you remember anything
as to his personal appearance on the occasion?' 'Yes, I
remember distinctly. His appearance was that of a
working man. He had on a short jacket, and looked
somewhat odd and unclerical.'"

The whole thing was unique. The preacher's singularly grotesque attire, vehement rousing eloquence, and striking personality, it would be simply impossible to describe.

The news of the sermon was soon abroad, and in a short time his services were sought for with eagerness far and near. At times the chapels were too small for the congregation, and the service was held on the village green. These exciting gatherings are still spoken of with enthusiasm by many who lovingly recall the grand scenes, the powerful times, the delighted audiences, but above all, the many conversions.

With the unmistakable mark of the Divine approbation upon him, the local preachers' meeting accepted and welcomed him in its brotherhood. In the midst of the comical, and, what perhaps in most cases would have been fatal, peculiarities of dress, manner, and speech, the real worth of the man was recognised, and, in due course, Peter's name was put on "full plan."

CHAPTER V.

Days of Triumph.

METHODISM does not know, and never can know, its indebtedness to its Local Preachers. Only a Local Preacher! Indeed; without him, thousands of services would have to be abandoned, the greater number of which have been brought into existence through his self-denying task; and it must not be forgotten that from his brotherhood every separated minister has been called to a wider, though not more honourable, sphere.

Peter's Sundays were now filled with a new kind of toil. Tramping many miles on his glorious errand, and only sustained by his young, passionate love for the Master who commanded him, it was no unusual thing for him to arrive home only in time to exchange his pulpit attire for the miner's garb. At times, there was a friendly lift by the way, and "anything with a wheel" would do for the self-forgetful man. His favourite quadruped was at times in request, but a horse was a rarity.

But the demands of the wide circuit were, after all, not entirely responsible for this extreme pressure. The fact is—and I wish to be faithful in this small book on a great man—Peter, like many of his order—his ministerial brethren have long ago grown out of such weaknesses—loved a little chat after the evening service; and what with the singing, the recounting of spiritual joys and triumphs, and the bit of "bird's-eye," the time went like magic, and the happy soul of the man was only brought back to mundane realities by the restless donkey at the door; or the more restless brethren who, almost wearied with waiting, conjured up visions of home and the pit shaft.

An amusing and characteristic story is told of a good day's work at Chester-le-Street. The good people listened to his marvellous words at first with prejudice and suspicion, but wonderment and admiration speedily bore down all silent objections. Quite a little crowd gathered about the preacher at the close of the day, and escorted him to the inn yard. It was too much state for the miner, who reflected on the homeliness of his dress, and the greater homeliness of his "turn out." But at length, when the collected bits of harness were satisfactorily arranged on the impatient steed, Peter, sitting on his cart, as if on a throne—there have been far more contemptible ones—cried, "Now, we'll have one verse more," and he led off with the rousing lines:

> "When he first the work began,
> Small and feeble was his day."

In after years, he playfully said, that if ever an account of his life would be required, there should be a delineation of him in the unpretentious chariot with the well-known verse to commemorate the day of small things.

It is refreshing to note that the enchanting stages of sudden popularity never "turned the head" or heart of

Peter. He was quite honest in his merry outburst. It was not in him to kick the ladder down, by whose help he rose. "Paint me as I am," said the great Cromwell to Lely; and the American President, who was not ashamed of the tailor's shears, is entitled to the respect of all who honour the sacred name of *man!*

There are scores of valuable and discriminating accounts of the preacher at this time, which throw light upon the growing power and remarkable success of "the man of the people."

From men of different moods and temperaments, I gather these testimonies. Of a memorable service says one: "It was a blessed time, and at the close of the service there was a rush—scores of penitents came forward in a few minutes." Says another: "Forty-five years have passed since he entered upon his evangelistic labours in the colliery district of Durham, but there are numbers yet to be met with who owe their conversion to his efforts; and many of them in turn have led, and are still leading, others to Christ. I have known many men engaged in this work, but never a more single-minded soul-winner than Peter Mackenzie was in those days."

Again, we have a characteristic incident reported from the Bishop Auckland Circuit, where on one preaching excursion he grew so excited as to break down the "crocket," or stool, on which he was standing. Turning to his no less excited congregation, he exclaimed, with marvellous self-possession, which at once revealed his ready wit and resources, "Kind friends, sing a verse or two till I mend my crocket."

The donkey again! Having the loan of an animal with which he was not on terms of personal intimacy, it transpired that the rider and his strange steed had different ideas about crossing a bridge, which stood between the preacher and his appointment. He says, "It would not go, so I took off my coat, wrapped it round its head, and then turned it round a few times, and so spoiled its geography. Then it went straight over." Thus the bewildered animal and the delighted preacher arrived at their destination.

How the pit men did idolize him, to be sure! Mr. Tweddle, of Stanhope, says: "The Rev. Peter Mackenzie, when a coal miner in the smoke-begrimed colliery district of North-East Durham, formed friendships and associations which he never forgot when he became a gentleman of the cloth. One in particular, now a rolleyman for the North-Eastern Railway Company at Wolsingham. They were chums: hail fellows well met. There was a school of men, a clique of friends, comrades, fellow-workmen, horny-handed sons of toil. In the battle of life these breadwinners got scattered in pastures new. One got to the old town of Wolsingham. Peter visited Weardale, and lectured and preached in Stanhope Castle Park. In the congregation was the rolleyman. Although years had intervened, the quick eye of Peter saw him in the crowd. As soon as the service was over he went for him, and gave him one of the heartiest shakes of hands he ever got in his life. 'How is ta, min?' said he, 'en hoo's the others?' mentioning his old comrades by name, one by one, with great glee. Said he, 'What rackets we had in the stables. Praise the Lord. Them was jolly times.' The rolleyman said, 'Aw thowt you would hev forgotten me!' 'Forgot tha! Why, man, aw nivvor forget a friend!'"

A very competent witness says of him in those days of the opening of a great public life: "He was blessed with a retentive memory, and a rare gift of imagination. Speaking of the impotence of all attacks against the truth of God, he said, 'Ye might as well try to knock down Durham Cathedral with a pop-gun;' and of the vision of God to those who pray, 'The saint upon his knees can see farther than the tip-toed philosopher through Rosse's telescope.' Again, of the might of angels, 'One of them could take the globe in the hollow of his hand, and skew it into the wilds of immensity, where neither man nor devil could find it any more.' Sameness could never be laid to his charge. He was fond of Bunyan, and some of the poets, and would sometimes quote Pollok by the page in the pulpit.'"

This reference to the gifted author of "The Course of Time" is to be noted as revealing the width and variety of Mackenzie's reading and taste at that early period of his public career. The man who can appreciate and appropriate Pollok, surely does not belong to the common run of men. Even then he was an observant traveller on the highroads of ordinary literature, but struck off into many a byway of tempting, precious knowledge, the results of which not only increased the value of his work, but enlarged the profit of his audiences, as it also excited their wonder and applause.

'A light of that kind could not be long "hid under a bushel;" or, as he once said, "without burning the

bottom out ; " and it is a matter of little wonderment
that the coming man was in universal demand for miles
round.   The chapels were simply packed when he
preached, and conversions were gloriously common—and
real.   The people were not only aroused, but *saved*.   All
round Bishop Auckland there linger sweet, glad testimonies to the spiritual power and success of the young
miner.   He carried all before him, and the ministers who
had charge of him, to their honour, helped and favoured
the untutored " local ; " yet a man upon whom the mark
of the Holy Ghost was set.

CHAPTER VI.

CALLED AND CHOSEN.

———

THE gold fever of 1851 disturbed many industrial centres in England, and the miners of the north were touched by its magic allurements, hundreds of whom emigrated in search of better fortune beyond the seas. The going forth had a great fascination for the young preacher, but a fortunate and unexpected difficulty arose, and, after a second attempt at emigration, he settled down reluctantly, for lack of means. The truth is, an unseen Hand was upon the man, and also upon the authorities of the Bishop Auckland circuit, who, with a rare insight into worth and character, resolved, in the usual formal way, to engage the services of Peter Mackenzie as a lay evangelist. Mr. Cooper, of Haswell Colliery, made things somewhat easy, so that the zealous young miner could meet at least some of the excessive demands made upon him; and the name of the under-manager is entitled to profoundest respect by all who knew the far-famed preacher in after years. Quoting from the small fragment of a diary which Peter wrote, Mr. Dawson gives us this extract:—

"Preached and worked in the Black Boy Colliery for six months. Was employed by the Auckland friends for

some four years. Saw three or four hundred brought in."
Surely not a bad record, even for my Lord of Durham
himself !

There are emphatic and reliable testimonies from very
different quarters regarding the rising man. An old and
venerated minister, Rev. Thomas M'Cullagh, under whose
"flag" I served in other days, often told the story, how
Peter stirred his circuit. That story has been in print,
but it will bear telling again and again :—

"In prayer meetings he agonized in oft-repeated
prayers, body and soul. When with him I have seen
vapour rising from his coat from the sweltering perspi-
rations of the strong, well-knit frame beneath. . . . .

" I found him athirst for information, and teachable.
One day he was in my study, looking through a small
volume of sermons, by James Parsons, of York, while I
was writing a letter. Addressing me, he asked if I would
lend him the book. I replied, ' I will make you a present
of it, if you will honestly confess for what purpose you
want it.' ' I want it,' said he, ' to get some plums for my
cake.' "

Yes, and how many sermon-cakes have been made,
without confession, out of the genius of such men as
Parsons, Jay, Spurgeon, Parker, and Talmage, not forgetting
the old Puritans and Anglican Divines—who can say?
This is an age of religious " tit-bits " to a sorrowful extent,
and the preacher who makes his sermon " out of his own
head " or heart, is somewhat rare, if his following is not.
Helps for the pulpit are plentiful enough, but many so-
called sermons are manifestly made on the plan of an
industrious, though scarcely honest, baker of Sunday

dinners, who made up his weekly repast by abstracting a portion from those of his customers, thus extending, if not enriching, his own Sunday banquet.

Says Mr. Thompson, of Middlesbrough, "I know when he had to come to my native village (Etherley) we looked forward with delight and great expectation for weeks to the approaching visit. I have seen the communion rail filled night after night with penitents seeking salvation . . . . and it was marvellous how he could win men and women over to Christ! As soon as he had done preaching, he came down out of the pulpit, and, jumping on to the forms with outstretched arms, he would cry, 'Come away to Jesus, hinnys; come away to Jesus, hinnys.' And when the prayer meeting ended, and we got outside, we formed a ring, and Peter got in the middle of it, when we had a grand sing which stirred the whole village. May I say here, that every night when he had finished the service, his clothes were wet through with perspiration, and he had everything to change when he got to his lodgings."

This kind of exhaustive service, maintained to the end, though afterwards in somewhat different methods of Christian endeavour, always produced the same physical results. In no sense was Peter Mackenzie "a *dry* preacher."

From the time—and indeed before—he was put on the circuit plan, he was more extensively popular, and signally owned as a soul-winner, than the brethren who honoured themselves in putting him there, and in his new and less fettered position, his remarkable natural gifts and spiritual power in dealing with the different

crises of the soul's experience, marked him out as a
heaven-sent messenger to the glad astonishment and
salvation of hundreds upon hundreds.

All that refers to those days is now a very precious
possession. Mr. Dawson says: " He became a sort of
religious stoker for the district, and wherever the fire of
spiritual life and activity had burned low, his assistance
was invoked to give it a new stir and fresh fuel." But the
pit-preacher was no less successful in winning souls than
he was in obtaining the "earthly treasure" in the
people's pockets. No church can exist or extend without
the just or generous gifts of its adherents. The just may
live by faith, but it is a difficult thing to reach the
unregenerate by means of that article only. True
Christians know that their great propaganda cannot be
advanced without " the gold and silver, and cattle upon a
thousand hills," of which their Master is Lord and
Proprietor, and of which they are merely stewards for the
time being. The great Christ was once almost penniless—
perhaps quite—and sent his friends to find funds in the
strange exchequer of a fish's mouth. Wesley knew the
power of pence; and there is a story told of Whitefield,
touching one of his memorable field-days on Kennington
Common, when he reached so many pockets, and so
deeply, because he touched so many hearts and con-
sciences (aye, there is the secret!), that it required the
services of two men and a wheelbarrow to remove the
collection.

Peter was always great at collections — great
collections—and it is a matter of curious interest to find
him so successful in his early preaching days; and as

gathering in the "shekels" forms no inconsiderable part
of a Methodist preacher's work, it may be worth recording
the testimony of the Rev. Joseph Hall, touching this
important matter.   Here are his words: "The people at
Sherburn Hill had a great day on Sunday.   Peter
preached morning and afternoon in a marquee, and in the
evening outside, as the crowd was so immense.   The
evening collection was so heavily weighted with copper,
that it required two men to carry the vessel in which it
was removed."

Was it any wonder that bewildered circuit officials,
and perplexed superintendents of poor, weak Methodist
interests, looked him up, and sought his kindly, but too
often generous, aid?

To his undying honour let it be recorded that he
never selfishly studied acceptable payable engagements,
but gave his invaluable services to poor struggling villages
and hamlets in preference, knowing that there he was
wanted most.   He might have died a wealthy man—and
so he did in the *love* of hundreds of thousands—but
following the early Methodist injunction, he always went
to those who needed him most.

It is hardly saying too much to remark that he was
in those days the "idol" of the people.   Anything that
Peter said or did was quoted or described with immense
enjoyment, and retailed as precious personal reminiscences
in after years.   Almost everything he said was considered
sacred, and treasured accordingly.

A sympathetic writer in the *Methodist Recorder* says:
"Whilst conducting a successful revival mission at the
village of Ramshaw, and the ceiling of the chapel being

low he raised his fist too high, and left an indentation in the roof. Because Peter had made it, it had to remain as a memento of his visit and work there, and for more than thirty years, to the writer's knowledge, it was referred to with pride, both by the preacher and people."

These successful promising and prophetic days clearly indicated a wider ministry, and the enthusiastic village evangelist heard at length the call of his Master and the church, and went forth to more extended fields of employment.

CHAPTER VII.

CALLED AND CHOSEN.

ONE who knows the Methodist history of the Bishop Auckland circuit best, says, "Such was the demand for his labours, it soon became evident that his future life would have to be spent in the work of proclaiming the Gospel. . . . . . His being married, having two children, and being thirty-two years of age, increased the difficulties of his getting into the ministry, and the inquiry was made whether he could not be engaged by the Conference as a lay agent. This, however, could not be done, as there was no provision for such a class of workers in the Connexion at that time, and, after much deliberation, it was resolved that he should be recommended as a candidate for the ministry."

So, in due course, Peter triumphantly passed the ordeal of the properly-jealous Quarterly Meeting. It is remarkable how ministers—his exact opposite in everything except godliness—took him by the hand. The superintendent of the circuit was the Rev. Richard Brown. The minister and the candidate stood far apart as the poles; but both knew Calvary, though they reached it by different tracks.

The inner life of the man may be judged by his own handwriting at that time, and which he could have had no idea would ever be put into print.

"Lord, help me!" he wrote. "My soul shall live for Thee alone. O, make me a man after Thine own heart! Stand by me, and, according to the ability that Thou hast given me, I will declare Thy will. I am Thine for ever; I feel it."

"Stand by me!" One is reminded of Luther, at Worms, when, anticipating appearing before the second conference of the great historical Diet, he paced his cell, or, kneeling on its stone floor, cried, "Stand by me! O, save me!"; and the quick, timely answer of victory came in due course, as all the world knows.

There is another glimpse. Dr. and Mrs. P. Palmer were making a great stir in the land with their holiness mission. The churches were edified, refreshed, lifted, by their efforts; but, from a book of the saintly, gifted woman's, "*Faith, and Its Effects*," Peter caught sight of the "Promised Land"—and he never lost it until Faith was "lost in sight," and he entered the Land and saw the King in His beauty. "Glory to God and the Lamb for ever!" he writes.

> "'Thou from sin dost save me now,
> Thou wilt save me evermore.'

"I do believe; and I do possess the land of rest from inbred sin, the land of perfect holiness. Glory! Glory! Glory!"

Candidates taught and moved thus by the Holy Ghost will always be a power for spiritual service to men, whether recognised by the necessary formalities of the Church or not.

Then Peter Mackenzie went up to London to stand before the dread tribunal of the July Committee, usually composed of the wisest and most experienced ministers the Methodist Church can command. It was not his first visit to the great " Modern Babylon." He had had a week of evangelistic work there, and made good use of his sight-seeing, as Mr. J. Reed, of London, tells us. On the return home, he preached, to a packed congregation of eager listeners, from the sweetly attractive words— " In My Father's house are many mansions." After a vivid description of the Crystal Palace, and even a more vivid description of Solomon's Temple, he exclaimed: " Look at them both again ! See them ! Grand as they are, compared with the mansion that Christ is preparing for us in the Father's house they are just like back pantries."

The Rev. W. Arthur has rendered splendid service to Methodism, but he never did a more effective thing for his Church than when he persistently stood by Peter Mackenzie in his London Examinations. But they must have been trying times for Peter. Mr. McCullagh says, " He sat first for his paper examination in Greek, Latin, French, English, mathematics, algebra, arithmetic, history, geography, &c. This was called the literary paper, after which came the theology paper. At the close, he hastened to my house. ' Well, Peter,' I asked, ' how have you got on with your paper ? ' ' Oh,' he replied, ' that literary paper ! She was hard ! I couldn't get in my pick at all ; but when I got to the theology paper, I was able to hew a bit.' ' What will you do if you are rejected ? ' I asked. ' I will go back to Bishop Auckland,' he replied, shouting ' Glory ! '" No doubt an unusual and unlikely experience of ecstasy for a rejected candidate, but the man was honest in the outburst of his faith in the Divine leading. The end of it was, Peter was accepted as a candidate for the ministry, Mr. Arthur closing a prolonged discussion by declaring, "It is my opinion that if you do not accept Mr. Mackenzie, you will commit a sin against God's Providence."

There are characteristic incidents belonging to that trying week in London. The son of the respected minister who was chairman of the Manuscript Committee for that year writes, "When he (Peter) heard that he and his sermon had been accepted, he took a cab from Westminster Training College, where the candidates were billeted in those days, and drove to Spital Square. Unusual sounds were heard as a head was thrust out of the window of the cab.—'Hallelujah! here we are! Stop, driver! Glory! Glory! Glory!' Then, when he stepped out, there was another shout of 'Glory! Hallelujah! Where is that blessed man of God? I have come to thank him for passing my sermon.'" The cabman has given us no idea of his strange fare, and London cabmen know a thing or two, but we may be sure, Peter, who afterwards travelled hundreds of miles in the familiar vehicle, which was no less a pleasure than a necessity, was never nearer heaven, when on wheels, in his life.

There is one other incident, where we find him on the octagonal of the college in company with a fellow candidate. Surveying the dense neighbourhood, with the multitude of house-tops, the thought of the swarming slums below caused him to seize the coat-collar of his friend and cry, "Down on your knees, brother Dixon," while at the same moment he himself knelt on the leaden roof, and poured out his soul in loud and earnest prayer for the perishing multitudes.

Thus it was that, in the order of things, Mackenzie transferred himself and his family to Didsbury, where comfortable quarters were found him, though not within the college buildings. He was, however, to have all the educational advantages the institution could confer, by means of its lectures and classes. Alas! such were of small use to him; though, no doubt, the one year he spent at Didsbury was greatly helpful to his inquiring mind. But the grave professors could make nothing of him. Perhaps it was as well. One says "he almost broke the hearts of his tutors, so 'dense' was he in his studies." Curiously looking at a Greek grammar, he was heard to say, with a suggestive look, "There isn't a word of Christ in it!"

But he was a Bible student, and the whole of his work—and increasingly so to the end—revealed a range of research and industrious preparation that fairly astonished the college community, as well as the crowded congregations which gathered to hear his message.

The Governor of the college, Rev. John Bowers, the President, who was, we are told, the very pink of propriety, a stickler for decorum, was wise enough to measure the strange new-comer aright, though he and many others must have been often strangely startled by Peter's excited outbursts; and often the sedate routine of scholastic order was disturbed by the joyous ejaculations of "Glory! Hallelujah!" when not unfrequently the old fire would burn up quickly in many a young

man's soul, and the sons of the prophets would flock
into some convenient room for a rousing prayer-meeting.
I do not know how it is managed now, but the thing
ought not to be a novelty in any college course.   "Who.
can forget," says an old fellow-student, "who heard his
exclamation in one of those meetings in the Assistant
Tutor's room—and he was very joyous :—'The devil
would rather stand neck-high in hell fire than be in a
good Methodist prayer-meeting.'"

Peter was only one year at Didsbury, or, rather, a
small part of the year, as the authorities could put
little into him, or, what perhaps was more satisfactory,
could take less out. Concerning those days there are
many characteristic incidents told by some of his old
fellow-students, many of which have had a wide circulation for years, but here is one that will bear telling
again :—On a certain morning the reluctant student was
absent from his classes, and the Governor, Mr. Bowers,
finding that Peter had gone down into the slums of
Manchester to preach the Gospel, followed him, and
found the truant standing on an old chair, preaching to
a miscellaneous congregation, much to their wonderment
if not their edification.   "Hallo! here comes Governor
Bowers," exclaimed the excited Mackenzie.   "Come
along here, Mr. Bowers; come and pray."   And the
head of the college did.

Said a venerated minister, in grave tones, to the fiery
young miner, "Mr. Mackenzie, why do you not clothe
your ideas in a more appropriate manner?"   It was no
use; Peter was ready with the unexpected answer, "Bless
the Lord, Doctor, they run off so fast, I haven't time

to clap a shirt on them!" We can well understand how dull the hours were to him when attending classes, and he said, when one made an inquiry regarding his getting on: "I could do better if I had a softer vein." As the years went on, he got his "pick" into many a "vein" and brought forth hidden treasure, to the great enrichment of multitudes.

What was to be done with such a man? The answer was, that in obedience to the manifest direction of Heaven, "Loose him, and let him go," he was permitted to wander forth on evangelistic excursions, to the immense spiritual profiting of the circuits that were fortunate enough to secure his services. The President's Assistant for that year, Rev. C. H. Kelly, had the unusual labour of answering one thousand letters—sometimes thirty in a day—praying that Peter might be sent to all kinds of needy interests.

Mr. Dawson gives interesting items from the evangelist's small diary, which reveal the significant and pleasing fact that, while his popularity widened, his piety deepened. And this was the universal testimony. During that broken, eventful year he was honoured in witnessing the conversion of one thousand souls—a record, perhaps, not even approached by a probationer in his first year's ministry before or since.

CHAPTER VIII.

The Years of Probation.

———

SO Peter began circuit life in the usual orderly way. If he could not be made to fit in with college methods, it was thought that a large, strong, typical circuit would be able to control and shape the fiery preacher. I never think of Mackenzie in those days, tied down to the routine of Methodist work and usages, without the suggestion of an eagle being confined in a hen coop, or a racehorse attached to a coal cart. The man was too big for any cramped ecclesiastical arrangement. God sometimes gives such men to the Church, and she does not know what to do with them. They cannot be tied down. Who can wonder that "General" Booth chafed under the, to him, galling, rigid routine of ministerial life, and the exactions of a multitude of small things every true, Heaven-sent evangelist ought to be free from? When William Booth left the Methodist New Connexion no doubt it was a great loss to that church, but it was an unspeakable gain to the whole world, such as no words can describe.

The Church has to learn, like every other institution; and as there was no "Forward Movement," such as we know it now, forty years ago, the authorities did what they considered wisest and best, and sent the difficult man into the thick of regular, methodical circuit work. Thus it was he came to Burnley. Outside his own familiar colliery districts, perhaps no town or neighbourhood could have been more suitable for the new start in life. The keen, shrewd, but warm-hearted people gathered round him at once. So much so that, even at five o'clock in the morning, the pit-preacher could command a congregation of a thousand workers, bound for the mill, the mine, or the forge, at a preaching service. And in ordinary the people thronged the chapels where Peter was announced, when conversions were many and wonderful, including some converts whose names rank high in the commercial world and official life of Methodism to-day.

In a letter to his staunch friend, Mr. M. Braithwaite, he gives a long account of his victorious progress. Speaking of one grand effort, he says, "I gave them the Thief. We bundled him up bag and baggage by the express, booking him right through; he never halted at Hell's Junction, nor put on brake at Purgatory, nor blew his whistle at Perdition, but went right to Paradise."

The subject of the Dying Thief is a striking and popular one, but the preacher's marvellously dramatic realism of the whole thing was unique. Peter's description of Hell's Junction I shall never forget. The crowds of demons, as he pictured them, waiting for the catastrophe of another lost soul, and their infinite amazement and chagrin as the salvation express shot by on the safe line to Glory, beggars all description. I heard the sermon in a great racing town, and particularly watched its effects on a little, demure solicitor who had never been seen to laugh or cry: but I noticed that when he came round with the collecting plate, he could hardly see what he was doing, for there were big tears in his eyes.

But somehow, the crowded chapels when Peter preached, the greatly swollen collections, and above all, the extraordinary additions to church membership, appeared out of joint with the old order, and whether the circuit officials, or Mackenzie's colleagues are to be credited with the decision, it would ill become me to say; but the inexorable command of the Conference made it imperative for him to " move on " at the end of one year's remarkably successful labour. No doubt the good Burnley officials did what they considered the right thing, but when Peter said good-bye to the stirring Lancashire town, he left behind him far more aching hearts than any other of his brethren have commanded, before or since.

Had Mackenzie been made of commonplace materials, the sudden and violent contrast which his new circuit— Monmouth—presented would have dismayed and disheartened him. Instead of ministering to vast crowds in the congested town, he had to wander weary miles among sparsely-populated hamlets. Long walking excursions to appointments, and dark, dreary returnings home by forests and moors, only served to bring out the Mark Tapley side of his cheery nature. Writing to an old friend, he says, "I have walked fourteen miles. Two souls saved. Hallelujah! I shall never have gout!"

But a benevolent lady came to his aid, and presented him with a smart white pony; and it was a sight indeed when Peter went down the streets of Coleford, where he was located, astride his charger, with his silk hat in his hand, which he occasionally rattled by his side in order to promote a more rapid progress. It may seem odd, but the ex-collier always had a weakness for silk hats, and was particular about their style, as he was also particular about his perfumery. These may be "small-beer chronicles," but we must have them, as such trifles make up and furnish the real man.

People of all social grades flocked to hear him when he occupied the pulpit of Monmouth Chapel, and the same spiritual force was manifest that had attended his ministrations from the beginning. Wet or dry, the people tramped in to hear him. It was a memorable time for the Monmouth circuit. All the funds were enlarged, and some new schemes greatly furthered. An amusing story is told of his ready wit in helping the friends out of a financial dilemma—no unusual thing in Methodism—where the promoters of a village chapel found that the cost of the structure had outrun their means. There was some dismay, and possibly some strong English words were employed; while the solemn document of the Manchester Chapel Committee would hardly bring any considerable comfort. " Well, never mind, friends," said Peter; "it's not a great mistake. He was told to order low shoes, and he ordered high-topped boots instead." This charitable view of, perhaps, a not uncommon weakness among inexperienced temple builders I respectfully submit to the Manchester Committee.

Two years were spent in the Forest of Dean, and then Mackenzie was transferred to the Melksham circuit, in Wiltshire. This was almost purely agricultural ground, and no doubt vividly recalled his Fifeshire days. But it must have been hard, exhausting work for the zealous preacner, strong as he was. Small villages, feeble churches, and long distances were no aids to encouragement, but he was faithful in little as in much. Says one who lived with him then: "His custom was to visit every house he could, and to pray with every family."

Long years ago, I heard at Salisbury accounts of the man's marvellously successful work. The country side was full of Peter Mackenzie; no wonder he was in constant request far and near. They tell a good story in the old city to this day, how that Peter, through being inveigled away from his circuit, failed to turn up at one of his appointments. The place in question was a small conventicle, on the edge of Salisbury Plain, but the dear people thought all the world of it. When Peter came on his next appointment, he was reminded of his failure. He cheerily announced at once that he would pay off old scores, and treated the delighted villagers to *two* sermons on en:l. The old Scotch country people were familiar with that kind of thing, but it must have been a new experience for the Wiltshiremen. However, the parties were "quits" to the satisfaction of both.

Let it be said, with all honour to the people of those villages in the Monmouth and Melksham circuits, they stood by their minister, and though they were unable to give much in cash, they gave largely in kind. They knew the man's worth, and loved him, and in many a thatched

cottage his name is fragrant to-day. There are many
pleasant glimpses of his innocent playfulness during those
hard years on the "Downs." It must have been real fun
to Peter when one night he had to join his brethren on
their way to a missionary meeting. With the spirit of
his old merriment within him, he suddenly waylaid them
at some unlooked-for place of meeting. "Your money or
your life!" was the awful gruff demand. The slash of
whip and plunge of umbrella, however, did the imaginary
highwayman no harm, who, quieting his somewhat
troubled colleagues, went on with them to complete the
missionary deputation.

In this way Peter faithfully went through his four
years of probation, and presented himself in due course
before the District Synod at Bath, for examination, before
being finally received as a member of the ministerial
brotherhood of the Wesleyan Church. The Rev. F. A. West
was the chairman—a "rasper," as Peter put it—and,
desirous of ascertaining the extent of the candidate's
knowledge of Christian themes, and his way of treating
them, the sedate, orderly minister asked Peter, in the
course of his inquiries, "What would you do with a Jew,
now, when opening out this matter?" To the surprise
and merriment of everybody, the ready answer was—as
the excited candidate stood forth dramatically, addressing
his venerable questioner, and eyeing him through and
through—"I should say, 'Now, Mr. Jew,'" &c. The
effect was irresistible; and in the end Peter was passed
on for ordination. There could be no other course.

CHAPTER IX.

——

RECEIVED into "full connexion" at the Conference of 1863, held at Sheffield, under the presidency of Dr. Osborn, Mackenzie was sent back North again to the coal pits and forges, among which his greatest triumphs had been won. There were two Haworths, brothers, in the ministry then, both saintly men, but Robert, Peter's superintendent in the Gateshead circuit, was a wonderfully genial, tender, large-hearted man, and, as one says, in the "sunniness" of his nature he was hardly second to Peter himself. Thus Mackenzie fell into good hands, and with wise, helpful, and generous guidance, plunged once more into the congenial work so dear to his heart, among thousands of men of his own old craft, and others.

It may be well to group the labours of the nine years which followed his ordination—years spent in Gateshead, Sunderland, and Newcastle.

The three years in the first of these circuits were eminently successful in every way. Everything went up by leaps and bounds. Four new chapels were projected, besides extensive alterations and enlargements being

entered upon.   In relation to one of these projects the
unselfishness of the man must be recorded to his honour.
Having promised to raise £100, he moreover generously
gave his watch to a colleague to be sold for the benefit
of the scheme.

It was not, as has been told, in the Gateshead circuit
but his next that the preacher fell among thieves one
dark night, who, however, had greatly mistaken their man.
Peter had never been a boxer, but he knew how to use
his hands, if not always in elegant fashion on the platform.
He saved his life and his purse in first-class style, and
arrived home with no more damage than his crippled
hat revealed.   Many substitutes came in to displace his
dilapidated head-gear, while more than one of the
preacher's assailants had something to think over for
days to come.   Yes, he had not forgotten the art of
"dusting jackets," when occasion required.

Those three years at Gateshead were very happy,
even triumphant ones.   The membership of the circuit
in 1865 was 839, and when he left for other labours it
was 1,500, with 200 on trial; and during the three years
£4,600 was raised for chapels and chapel debts.

No wonder the good people were loth to part with
him.   At a memorable farewell tea-meeting his generous
colleague and biographer read some verses, often printed
since, for which he offers modest apologies.   He need
not do that.   They are very pleasant, as showing not
only the gifted preacher, but the Christian unselfishness
of his brethren, who only felt themselves honoured by
being associated with him.   My little book will not
allow the introduction of all the stirring verses, but

here are some of them. Mr. Dawson brought unconscious honour to himself when, among other good things,
he wrote :—

> "Who was it came to Gateshead town
> When the Methodists were looking down ;
> Yes ; came without his bands and gown?
> 'Twas Peter.

> "Who filled the chapels very soon,
> Both in the country and the 'toon,'
> And put the people into tune?
> 'Twas Peter.

> * * * * * *

> "Who is it that, when far away,
> We'll think about for many a day ;
> And for his weal and welfare pray?
> 'Tis Peter.

> "Who is that, beyond the skies,
> We hope to see with gladdened eyes,
> Amid the light that never dies?
> 'Tis Peter."

The seventeen verses may be found in Mr. Dawson's
"Life of Peter Mackenzie," a work to which I here
respectfully submit my formal, but thankful, obligations.

Very characteristic and precious are the reminiscences of the Rev. W. Calvert, who saw not a little of
the home life of the famous preacher at that time. He
brought the circuit needs to the family altar, and prayed
for each place and its special wants. Mr. Calvert reveals
the playfulness of the man when he says, referring to a
drive with Mackenzie :—"Whilst putting his pony 'out'
the enthusiastic Jehu said, 'If John Wesley's doctrine
of the resurrection of animals be correct, and if the
laws of Heaven permit, I will have a race with Michael,
the archangel, on the plains of Heaven!'"

Yes, he was a good, safe, though dashing, whip; a fact he demonstrated one night to a timid friend, who was riding with him. "Don't be afraid, brother," he cheerily said, as he saw his companion's alarm at the unaccustomed pace; "you are as safe as if you were sitting in Gabriel's arm-chair!"

It was not a long remove to Sunderland, where for superintendent Mackenzie had no less a man than the eminently-gifted and gracious Thomas Vasey. Humanly speaking, no circuit could have been better "manned," and hope ran strong and high. But it was the time of ebb to a great revivalistic movement that had, in a sense, exhausted the people; and, alas! some sort of reaction had set in. No doubt the churches should always live at fever heat; but, so long as human nature remains what it is, there will come that inevitable reaction. Successive stirring methods bring, I do not say a natural after-depression, but, still, a quiet longing for the more settled service. No one can be blamed for this. Surely not Thomas Vasey, of all men! Surely not his devoted colleagues!

It is a solemn, but somewhat curious, study to note how the same sower, with the same seed, realises such different results to his labour. No doubt our Lord's parable on this matter affords not a little enlightenment. There was, however, no diminution of Peter's fire, force, genius, and industry—we have this on all hands; but the years spent in Sunderland were, to him and his superintendent, years of comparative disappointment. Not that the years were a failure: by no means; but the high tide of expectation did not reach the longed-for levels. It is gratifying to know that old Sans Street Chapel, then dwindling, owing to constant removals, like many others of its class, is now, under wiser and more spirited enterprise, renewing its youth, and, with a freer hand, bids fair to rival its old, best days.

One of the most pleasant things I have to write is that touching the patient, loving, and discriminate estimate and handling of the man by his senior brethren, who, in their work, were as far removed from their strange colleague as the Poles are from the Equator. But they knew the goodness and worth of the man, and, above all, his transparent honesty.

In his next circuit, Newcastle, he was still in touch with the miner's life; but his fame was broadening out among many counties. Though he had one free week in three for his extended excursions, he made it a point to turn up at the weekly ministers' meeting. However he managed to meet circuit duty and outside demands I cannot conceive; but he did. Here is a record week:—Writing to a dear friend, he says, "I am so hard pulled at, that it is quite a charity to let me alone. What would you think of three services in Newcastle, two in Yorkshire, two in Wiltshire, two in Dorsetshire, and one in Bristol, all in one week?" And this was the speed he went at until he broke down on the Leeds railway platform, and his Bible and "Bradshaw" were laid aside for the "rest that remaineth."

After a hard, good day at York, on one occasion, I joined the midnight mail from the north. As the express steamed in, Mackenzie's head appeared at a carriage window. He had had three services in Newcastle, and was bound for some far western villages two hundred miles away, but when I left him at Milford Junction he was as blithe as a lark, and as full of song.

Some idea of the extraordinary demands made upon the popular preacher may be gathered from a characteristic letter he wrote to a dear friend of mine, Mr. W. A. Millward, of Newton Heath, about this time. It is too good to omit. Here are some extracts:—" When I got here yesterday morning I found the Philistines in great force. I had only two hours, but I drew up my reserved list, and slaughtered one-third of the fresh army; the others, occupying a strong position, I had to leave in possession of the field. I again returned to the charge this morning, but their numbers having increased during the night I was compelled to employ an electric battery, four hundred miles long, which blew, as you may suppose, a number into the waste-paper basket."

This may seem a somewhat comic way of looking at the awful pressure put upon him, but it has a very tragic side to those who knew what the extra toil demanded and meant.

There can be no doubt that his nine years by the Wear and the Tyne were eminently successful, but the clamorous calls for his services all over the country interfered with and lessened his more direct evangelistic labours. New methods of presenting the same old truth had opened out to him, but in the new channels the same old spiritual force made itself apparent, and the growing anxiety to share in the famous preacher's development as a brilliant lecturer, for more than one reason, spread far and wide.

CHAPTER X.

Circuit Work.

—

NINE years in the manufacturing town of Leeds and district followed ; but it is only a mere glimpse I can give of that eventful, crowded period.

The authorities of St. Peter's circuit, Leeds, were no doubt thankful and jubilant in obtaining the services of Mackenzie, but though he could fill their vast central chapel at times, and in a great measure clear off its financial obligations, the permanent results of spiritual and constant labour such as the peculiar demands of the district required were not manifest. In a terribly congested neighbourhood, immeasurably lowered socially, and with a preponderating population of Jews and Roman Catholics, not to speak of tramps and wayfarers, how could the " travelling preacher " make any deep or lasting impression ?

It is pleasant to note in this connection that St. Peter's, like other great Leeds chapels, is wonderfully alive to-day. "The old order changeth," and it is an unmistakable sign of business-like sanity, when "live men" are settled down with a free hand to deal with such

E

forlorn neighbourhoods and deserted chapels. I turned
into the dear old place the other night, and with thankful
joy noted over a thousand worshippers of the right sort,
gathered by the magnetic influence of the genial pastor
and his valuable lay colleague.

Peter was faithful to his circuit demands, though
now and then it required a gentle, but strong, hand in
assisting him to restrain his generous instincts. It must,
however, have been hard work at times to say "No" to
the beseeching applications for his services. To one
urgent correspondent he writes:—"I am hard fast. I
don't know what to do. Our new chapel is opened, and
we have to work it as best we can. The "super" has
brought me four hundred tickets to renew. I have
collected for the cause this week, by eleven services,
over £180. It is rather too bad to shut me up for the
most of six weeks." Again, he writes:—"I have only
one day out for a fortnight, and that is on a Friday."

Peter Mackenzie occupies a place all his own in
the Methodist Church. Though known so far and wide,
he took little part in its complicated and multitudinous
affairs, though he was faithful personally, or by
generously-treated deputy, in attending to his circuit
work. He rarely attended Conference; though I remember him once, quite out of his element in the great
assembly in London, years ago, saying, with indescribable
but truthful emphasis, "She goes slow." No; he was
no Conference man; was never nominated for the
"legal hundred"; was never, to my knowledge, placed
on any committee, which are plentiful enough; never
had any official vote of thanks, which are more plentiful

still. His voice was seldom heard in a District Synod. He wrote no book; and never rushed into print in the papers. The only official recognition of the man was in his being appointed a member of a deputation for the Cornwall District, a lively account of which is given by the Rev. Joseph Nettleton. The whole thing is intensely amusing. Peter introduced himself as "the brown bread" of the deputation, on which Mr. Nettleton would spread his "Fijian butter," after which Mr. Marmaduke Osborn would cover it with his "marmalade." The Cornish people talk of that memorable deputation to this day.

Let a superintendent minister bear testimony regarding those Leeds days. Says the Rev. John Reacher :— "No tenderer, no truer man have I ever known. His pastoral visits to the sick were marked by rare insight and sympathy; and when the sick were also poor he was a cheerful giver."

During long years of acquaintance I never heard him complain of being "Mondayish." The word is not, I think, in the very latest dictionary, but the thing signified is common enough in some clerical circles. I never heard of his taking a "back-end of the week," or having a downright real rest and holiday. No doubt he had such breaks, but the painful, persistent, and clamorous appeals for his services chained him down like a galley-slave, and

"Now the labourer's work is o'er,"

he enjoys the well-earned rest his church could not afford him here. In the long repose, he sleeps quietly, and will for ever. Said an engine-driver on the North-Western, "I always think of him as I run through Dewsbury; I have driven him scores of times"; and the weather-beaten, intelligent man evidently felt as proud of his achievement as if he had been speaking of Royalty—perhaps more so.

In his next circuit, the same awful strain went on. The pace was killing; as he tried to crowd into a week the work of two—more, even. There are references in his brief letters, at this time, to the early love of the preacher's life. Says he: "We had a glorious time here (Leeds) last night, many seeking Jesus!" Again: "Some seeking the Lord, and in such earnest!"

It is noteworthy to observe how the lecturing and preaching were in no sense antagonistic in those days. When on a stray excursion to Padiham, he writes: "The Holy Ghost came down, and the gift of tongues was surely granted. One lady when she got mercy, stood up, and such a shout—'I'll praise my Maker while I've breath.' Oh! had you seen the hands held up to Heaven, the beaming face, the tears that tell the sins forgiven!" At the close of the letter there is a sadly pathetic and prophetic postscript: "I am afraid that the people will kill me before three years." We speak of some men being made of oak, but surely this man must have been made of angle iron, or he would have assuredly closed his marvellous labours when in the Leeds circuits.

The same fearful pressure was experienced in his new circuit, Shipley. Regarding his relations to his friends there, there is one very suggestive reference that he makes in after years:—"Tell Mrs. Holden I have never needed or taken anything since she brought me out, three years come May. . . . . ." Peter refers here to the "Blue ribbon."

In this connection, I well remember his coming to dine with me in Liverpool. He had had a long, tiresome journey, and as the dear lady of the house suggested some refreshment, remarking, "You must feel like sinking, Mr. Mackenzie," the tired traveller, pointing to his bit of blue, said, with quick, respectful animation, "No, madam, since I got this it has been all rising." The firm, but eminently gentlemanly, tone in which the wearied man said this was such as to cause the whole dinner-table to honour him.

So the three years in Shipley came and went, every day of which was crowded with incessant work. The Rev. F. R. Bell gives us a peep at the great traveller, who was his colleague in those days. "After dinner on Saturday I now and again made my way to his house, to assist him with his correspondence. It was his habit to throw his letters on the floor in the study when completed, and then, at the end of a long spell, he would say, 'Now, count them up. How many do you make of it?' Then the bell would ring for his daughter to get him five shillings' worth of stamps, and put them on, with, 'Lick them well, hinny; lick them well'; and after that it would be—'Now, just sit a bit, to show there is no animosity,' and he would light his pipe, and we would talk about the work he loved so dearly."

In due course Mackenzie removed to Dewsbury, where he was received with "open arms." This was his last circuit, and it may not be inappropriate to quote the words of Mr. D. K. Lobley, one of his executors, regarding the great preacher. The words are

discriminately weighed, and are valuable in the extreme,
as showing the devotion and love of the preacher for
his dear old work.   Says Mr. Lobley :—" His sermons
were strong appeals, deep in thought, sound in theology ;
and though his humour kept running out of his finger-
ends, the principal object he had in view was the
conversion of sinners and the building up of the church.
In the prayer-meeting which followed the Sunday
evening services he is still remembered with very great
joy by many of his friends he came in contact with.
It was in such meetings he was seen to best advantage.
He threw his whole large soul into them, and one felt
like Peter, James, and John on the Mount, for he
seemed to take one right within the gates of heaven."

CHAPTER XI.

THE TRAVELLING SUPERNUMERARY.

THEN Peter Mackenzie settled at Dewsbury as a supernumerary minister, to the great joy of the officials and good people of the circuit. The full record of his life in these circuits must be sought elsewhere, perhaps most and best of all in his hurried, child-like correspondence. But as no circuit was large enough for his coveted and invaluable services, he acted wisely in freeing himself from circumscribed circles for the vast and varied demands which the entire Methodist Connexion made upon him. When a minister becomes a supernumerary, he is often dubbed by the painfully graphic but often untrue phrase, "Worn out." There is a Worn-out Methodist Ministers' Fund, and a very righteous Fund too; but it must be a surprising and painful thing to many an educated and sensitive man, who yesterday was a superintendent of a large circuit, to find that to-day he is only recognised as a "Worn-out." Is there not sufficient ingenuity and charity—no, not that! plain common sense—in the Church to find some place for its very best men, and—perhaps at their best—putting them, say, on half-pay; and, instead of suddenly turning them into nobodies, wisely retain their ripened wisdom and experience for service that would gladden and enrich the most intelligent congregations?

But Peter Mackenzie was yet in his full strength, and it must have been a laughably amusing denomination of "worn-out" minister when he started off on his more extended excursions which meant the work of at least three no ordinary men. To a man of his temperament and toil, the trammels of circuit life and routine must have been intolerable, but very seldom did any irritation manifest itself, as he bravely faced the multitudinous demands made upon him for service at home or away. As we look at things now, our only regret is that he did not obtain his freedom years before. But the welcome relief came at last, and at the Conference of 1886 he was left with a free hand. The great kindness of the Dewsbury people and their neighbours must not be unrecorded here, as the new house of the travelling supernumerary was fitly furnished by their thoughtful and sensible generosity.

For most men of his years and work it would not have been too much to count upon *some* rest and leisure. But it was not to be. His Fridays were even in demand, and eager deputations were willing to snap at his Saturdays. If the gifted, popular man expected any quietude, he must have been terribly mistaken. The slavery to Connexional demands was more manifold and urgent.

The record of Peter Mackenzie's travel during those years—1886-1895—certainly far outdistanced that of any "travelling preacher" of his day, and was more than sufficient to dismay even the oldest "commercial" on the road.

Mr. Dawson gives a remarkable, but sadly pathetic, letter Mackenzie wrote to his old friend, Mr. R. Stevens, about this time. It reveals, in a more vivid light than any studied words can describe, the awful pressure that was put upon the man. "He sat down"—did he? Here is an extract from his cheery letter, which will speak for itself. In the scores of letters Mr. Dawson favours us with, we cannot but be struck with the extensive mileage covered by the "popular" minister. With ten or twelve services a week for ten years, he was in evidence in all parts of the kingdom. Peter writes :—"Dear old friends like yourself have written for me to go spend a week or two, and let them have a Sunday and a Monday; but it is no use—all is gone." Then follows a jumble of geography, suggesting an index to a railway guide, and almost enough to bewilder a railway expert—but Peter was well up in his "Bradshaw," and, perhaps, knew the "iron roads" better than any other man. Here is his list:—"The Isle of Man, and Cornwall, Bristol, Birmingham, Leeds, London, Liverpool, Manchester, Nottingham, Leicester, Luton, Darlaston, Workington, Berwick, Newcastle, Sunderland, Norwich, Lowestoft, Yarmouth, Outwell, Ashby-de-la-Zouch, Winsford, Sandbach, Burton, Bridlington, Scarborough, Filey, Driffield, Beverley, Hull, Barton-on-Humber, Gainsborough, Lincoln, Market Rasen, Exeter."

Let a man of ordinary intelligence, and of even more than ordinary travel, look at the map of England,

and imagine what this programme meant and involved! Think of it! Isle of Man and Cornwall; Sunderland and Norwich; Market Rasen and Exeter! There is no mention of Nova Zembla or Timbuctoo; but the fearful pace at which the great speaker was hurried about the country only affords one more illustration—and a very sorrowful one—of the folly of killing "the goose that lays the golden eggs."

Distance presented no difficulty to the restless, energetic man; and, really, it is marvellous to find how minute and correct his knowledge of railway matters was. Main lines, branch lines—he knew them all; and could manage to rush from Norfolk to Devonshire, in time for his *afternoon* work, in a manner that would fairly bewilder the experienced traveller.

If the wonderful preacher kept the list of his travels and engagements, it would be a thing of astonishment if allowed to get into print. But the physical resources of the strong, willing man had their limits, and there are many pathetic references in his letters, during the year 1895, to failing strength. His dear friend, Mr. Dawson, says feelingly, but truthfully, "Of mental vigour there was not a trace of decay, but the outer walls of the tabernacle gave signs, here and there, of yielding to the strain. What a cruel strain it was! It cannot be defended." Who does not share in the righteous indignation of his biographer, when he says: "Think of a man, of nearly seventy years of age, having thirty-eight services—and services such as his—without a break! There *must* and *ought* to have been some way of escape."

Poor Thomas Hood, who loved a jest, "within the
limits of becoming mirth," made fun out of his own
sorrow and pain and toil, on to the very end; and the
sportive humour of Peter was equally impressive as it
was unconscious. To a lady friend who invited him to
rest at her house for a few days, he made answer:
"There will be no rest for Peter Mackenzie, till he is
dressed in a wooden suit, and tucked in with a shovel."
To another, who asked him when he was going to give
up work, the reply was, "When I drop." I cannot
laugh at this. It is only a matter for tears.

He was literally chased down to Jordan by the
clamorous and unyielding importunities for service. I
never heard of him having a holiday run to the States, a
month down the Mediterranean, or a week in Wales. Yes;
he now and then had a "week-end," say, at Blackpool, but
he was in the Prince of Wales' Theatre on the Sunday.
He knew little of the dear people who think so much of
Keswick, Southport, and Grindelwald Conventions; but
a good, honest month of rest and quiet at any one of
those charming resorts would have brought days of
heaven on earth to the tired man, and maybe we should
have him now.

It was when serving the interests of village
Methodism, at Sheepshed, that the vigorous man broke
down somewhat, having taken cold. Let that be
affectionately noted: he was serving a *village*. The
following day he was at Bolton; the next at Longton,
in Staffordshire; and then, on the twenty-sixth of
October, ill as he was, he started off for Worcester.
The rest is soon told. We follow him to Winchcombe

(from which place he was driven, alas! in an open conveyance, to Cheltenham), thence to Reading, and on to Southampton. Again we follow him, travelling north to Darwen, taking Banbury on his way.

But the strong, willing man gave out at last. He was expected at Newcastle by hundreds of old friends; but the brave, generous soul would see the familiar Tyne no more. He reached Leeds; but could go no further. His second daughter took him home to Dewsbury, and thus terminated the "journeyings oft" of the marvellous traveller. He had nearly three years' engagements in his book; but there was one he was always prepared for, though for it he had no fixed date, and that was the long-looked-for interview with "The King in His beauty," and in Whose presence he would find his well-earned and long-sought rest.

CHAPTER XII.

———

WHEN the Great Master calls His servants to account it is well for them to be in readiness. No one knows, save the men themselves who are called to live and move in the glare, and among the cruel demands, of a popular ministry, what strict enforcements are necessary to the retaining, and development, of personal godliness. The whole thing—excited crowds; social, but often exacting, kindnesses; late hours—any hours (the good people want all they can get out of the honoured visitor); early trains; frequent open conveyances; many changes at railway points; stand-up dinners at refreshment counters, where there is often more glass than meat—is dangerous in more senses than one. The Methodist people little know what price their best men are required to pay. The pace is too quick for some, and they go under. But William Morley Punshon said, at the end of his exhausted life—much of which had been spent on railroads and ocean steamers—"Jesus is a precious *reality* to me now." And the miner preacher was with him in that matter. Many a good-hearted, brave, self-forgetful man has got stranded, somehow, in the currents of ceaseless professional labours; and the people who used to "hang on his lips" leave him in loneliness to meditate on the dismal truth—"They made me the keeper of the vineyards; but mine own vineyard have I not kept."

Everything was done. that love and professional skill could suggest or command; but the end had come at last. In his final letter he says, in his own genial way, "I am in the dry dock." But no amount of overhauling and repairing could be of use to him. His unsurpassed record voyages were finished, and the splendid craft was fit only for the inevitable break-up which, sooner or later, comes to us all.

Regrets are useless now. But, oh, if he had only had the wisdom and resolution to say "No" to scores of his friends, he need not have gone home to die at Dewsbury so soon.

As the closing scenes drew nigh the man who had edified thousands was supported in his prostration by the great themes he had so joyously discoursed. They were no cunningly-devised fables. He had been no dealer in *unfelt* realities, and the long-tested truth he had preached so variously, and so often, held him up and comforted him. Away from the stir and blaze of public excitements, it is beautiful to note the dying man gathering himself up, and saying, "I have had a happy life, bless the Lord, and I have enjoyed it. I am firm on the Rock." His irrepressible humour was manifest even to then. To his daughter

Janet he said, "Cheer up; I am better than two dead ones yet." He longed to preach again, but that form of service was past; but, "though dead, he yet speaketh."

The ruling passion held the preacher to the last, and even in his broken, disturbed slumber he was collecting materials for a new sermon on the sweetly-enticing words: "Thine eyes shall see the King in His beauty." What the vision was, will never be known here, but after some moments of collectedness he pronounced the great apostolic benediction: "The grace of the Lord Jesus Christ, and the love of God, and the communion of the Holy Ghost, be with you all," and then Jordan was passed, and in the better country, and in its unfading brightness, he saw his Master and King. He died on the 21st of November, 1895, in the seventy-second year of his age.

There was *something* in the papers the following day, when with various brief comments the death of the widely-known and beloved man was announced. The mournful tidings sent a thrill of sorrowful regret over the entire Methodist Connexion, and far beyond. Men whose lives are spent for the most part with coal, iron, cotton, or "shoddy," could only talk of one thing, and there were not a few tearful eyes on 'Change as the name of the gifted preacher was recalled.

Dewsbury probably never saw such a funeral as that that went forth when the mortal remains of the great traveller were laid to rest. Long before the advertised time for the memorial service, in his own old chapel, the building was crammed, and many hundreds were unable to obtain admission. Friends from all parts

of the country, including many ministers, came to honour
their old minister and comrade. It was an awfully trying
time when the coffin was placed in front of the communion
rails, the place of salvation to not a few who were
tearfully looking on at the mournful pageant. The
brethren in charge of the service, with bowed heads and
full hearts, showed how much they missed and mourned
their lost friend; but I may perhaps be pardoned if
I indicate the remarkably choice, discriminating, and
faithful estimate of Peter Mackenzie which Professor
Banks gave, in his own quiet, dignified, and measured
sentences. I am indebted to the *Methodist Times* for
the report of those memorable utterances. No two men
could be more dissimilar than the college professor
and the collier preacher, and it is a matter of immense
satisfaction to note how the scholarly Chairman of the
Leeds District could appreciate and acknowledge the life-
work of a man whose moods and methods were in
most respects so unlike his own.

"The name of Peter Mackenzie," said Professor
Banks, "had long been a familiar one with all branches
of the Methodist Church. He was a man by himself;
he belonged to no class, he followed no model, and he
could have no successor. He belonged to the ranks of the
exceptional men whom God raised up from time to time,
in the history of His Church, for special work. The
Church needed such men, just as it needed ordinary men,
and the Church that was without them was very poorly
equipped for doing God's work. The Church which had
them and did not know how to use them was narrow
and unwise. We were told that to the Apostolic Church

Christ gave apostles, prophets, evangelists, pastors, and teachers. Pastors and teachers were the most numerous, essential, and useful, and have formed the prominent order in the life of the Church, but the exceptional forms of service were mentioned first. Methodists, in looking back on the history of their Church, were thankful they had that feature in common with the New Testament Churches, that while they always possessed pastors and teachers, they had had men with special gifts for service. They had their John Nelsons, their David Stoners, their John Rattenburys, their Punshons, and their Peter Mackenzies. They had also had their Adam Clarkes, Richard Watsons, Jabez Buntings, and their Dr. Popes, and at the head of all—John Wesley. To these the inspired description applied, 'By the grace of God I am what I am.' Mr. Mackenzie could have used those words; no one had a better right than he. On the lips of the apostle they meant that God chose him from the first for special work. All the circumstances of his life worked together to prepare him for it. But Paul was typical of those servants of Christ who, not in great numbers, were raised up to do special work. They thanked God for men like Mr. Mackenzie; for his popularity, which was genuine, whatever any one might say to the contrary. It was won by honest means and used for the most unselfish and generous ends. The power to speak straight to the nation's heart was God's special gift to His chosen servants. It was not difficult to discover the sources of Mr. Mackenzie's great popularity. There was his humanness. He never merged the man in the minister. When speaking in God's name he was the opposite of formal, official, and conventional. There was about him robust manliness, but combined with it the most womanly and delicate tenderness. They would never forget his racy mother-wit. He saw at a glance what some only found out by the slow process of analysis, and put it before people in phrases and sentences that would not be forgotten. He was a magnificent master of assemblies in all things allied to human need, smiles and tears, joy and sorrow, and his power to touch the heart proved him to belong to the class of exceptional men. There was an indefinable attraction about his personality which could not be put into words, though every one could feel it. Mr. Mackenzie had it. In the early years of his ministry he was a mighty evangelist, and had he continued in that line might have been another David Stoner or John Rattenbury; but in his later days his steps were directed into another form of service. He had specially ministered to the needs of weak and struggling churches through the length and breadth of the land. His labours were enormous. Only an iron constitution could have enabled him to do the work he did. No one knew the amount of unselfish service rendered in this way. The providence of God had determined the time and manner of his end. It was more merciful to him than a lingering period of inactivity. His last words were the apostolic benediction. There could be no doubt it was his. His work was of an extraordinary character. But his sorrowing friends and the sorrowing Church could say, 'The Lord gave and the Lord hath taken away; blessed be the name of the Lord.'"

The procession was re-formed, and with the streets lined by mournful spectators made its way slowly to the cemetery. There Rev. J. Martin (the present superintendent of Dewsbury circuit) and Rev. John Smith (the late superintendent) divided the service between them, and in the presence of thousands of friends all that was mortal of Peter Mackenzie was laid to rest until the resurrection morning.

There were many choice and brightly-suggestive wreaths laid upon the "last of earth," but for pathetic significance the one sent by the cabmen of Dewsbury held a first place.

It may almost seem a waste of time and space to attempt a description of "Peter the Great," as he was affectionately styled. His broad-set, burly figure and well-shaped head; his merry, knowing, twinkling eyes, and endless varieties of facial expression, were known all over the country. Mr. G. H. J. Dutton communicates a somewhat exhaustive, but singularly graphic, phrenological delineation of the preacher to the columns of the *North-Eastern Weekly Gazette*, a clever paper, whose desire to gather and authenticate everything relating to the illustrious Mackenzie is beyond all praise.

Mr. Dutton says:—"The leading powers of his mind were his imagination, wit, imitation, and activity. His mind was literally crowded with ideas, and he had uncommon talent to amplify, embellish, and expand to an almost indefinite extent any subject he took up. His imagination was almost too active, and must have led at times to extravagance of statement, common to what the late Earl of Beaconsfield called 'a sophistical rhetorician.' Whatever faults he had were transparent, and chief among them must certainly be placed the tendency to exaggerate. His was a comprehensive mind: he could take in the whole Bible for a text, and present its truths in a nut-shell; or he could take a simple text, and expand it to any extent. One of his chief characteristics was his sense of the ludicrous. His love of fun and jokes, his ready wit, and his aptitude for seeing the funny side of everything, largely contributed to his success. Some have strongly objected to his 'lack of restraint,' but he could no more check the spontaneous flow of mirth and exuberance of spirits than Canute could keep back the flowing tide."

Summing up, the clever expert says:—" His was a complex nature, containing as it did imagination and practicality, reflection and observation, refinement and vulgarity, humour and pathos, passion and patience, humility and confidence, faith and reason, conservatism and radicalism. He must have had great temptations, but his sincerity helped largely to keep him steadfast."

To all who really knew Peter Mackenzie this analysis must commend itself as strikingly true. Elsewhere I refer to the methods of his looking at the truth, of which he was so renowned an expositor, and his modes of presenting it ; and to their consideration, and the character of the man himself, I must now pass on.

CHAPTER XIII.

PETER MACKENZIE was a "child of nature," and of grace. The two things need not be brought into any kind of conflict. Regeneration does not undertake the entire reconstruction of a man. It only checks and ends the springs of moral evil, but retains and employs in the new service the old mental and physical tendencies and characteristics. So it is not difficult to imagine how another Peter would retain his old demonstrative bearing after his searching and painful probation, and how the eager Saul continued the same enthusiastic man, when in after years he carried the "fiery cross" of the great crusade round about even unto Illyricum. The old characteristics remained, but were glorified when the one thundered in the streets of Jerusalem, and the other took his place on Mars Hill.

Peter Mackenzie was an eminently good man, and, though he never advertised himself as such, carried the evidence of the fact wherever he went and into whatever he did. The dainty scent of a ripe clover field requires no notice board to draw attention, and the worth of the man needed no ostentatious proclamation.

Mr. Dawson says:—"Those who knew him well before his conversion describe him as the embodiment of mirthfulness, and what religion did was to soften this instinctive hilarity into a gracious vivacity without rendering it a whit less natural. And as with cheerfulness, so with all the other qualities of his nature; by a wholesome piety all were fashioned to sweeter uses, none of them maimed or extinguished."

Peter Mackenzie was, all through his course, a man of prayer. That was his great secret. In the seclusion of a first-class railway carriage he found his oratory, and many a railway man knew that when he had closed the carriage door he had shut the traveller in with his God. People wondered how he could turn up so bright and fresh after long, tiresome journeys, and after the singing of some favourite hymn—perhaps his old love:

"My heart and voice I raise," &c.,

enter with spiritual zest into the holy exercise of prayer. There was a strange, charming simplicity about it all; no stale, stock religious phrases or irrelevant Scriptural allusions. He was so often at the Mercy Seat on his own account, and for the needs of others, that he was never far from its neighbourhood, and indeed it was never out of sight. The usual thing for him to do was, on crossing the threshold of every house, to fall on his knees and supplicate the benediction of Heaven, sometimes to the astonishment of his hosts who were unfamiliar with his methods.

It was the man's habit to take "*everything* to God in prayer." Let one testimony stand as an illustration of many hundreds. Says a gentleman who often entertained him:—"On his arrival, Mr. Mackenzie would have prayer with us, after which we allowed him as much privacy as we could." From all sorts of association with him I know this was no occasional impulse, but the spiritual and confirmed habit of his life. Though a born actor, he was beautifully unconscious of it, so that his innocent sportiveness often peeped out in his very prayers, and the pulpit prayer was as often acted as offered. In any other man the whole thing would have been disgustingly abhorrent, but the people knew the genuineness of the man, who, in spite of unaccustomed words and gestures, got them nearer to God and heaven.

Here are some scraps which no one can use or imitate. At fashionable Brighton his congregation were startled by the vehement outburst—"Lord, save the Methodists, for they are running after the Independents; Lord, save the Independents, for they are running after the Church of England, for she is running after the Church of Rome; Lord, save the Church of Rome, for she is running after the Devil." The description of the mad race will not easily be forgotten. Of course the outburst was novel and striking, but Peter Mackenzie only put, in his direct homely way, the situation of things about which other good men think and speak and fear, though in a more involved and roundabout fashion. But I do not pretend to hold any brief for the great preacher in this matter. He was once holding a service on a

windy day, and in the generousness of his nature put in
a petition for "the old women who had to stop and
hold on to their bonnet strings."

Here are other scraps.   At the opening of a new
Chapel, he remembered the trustees—a class of gentlemen
not often made the subject of special prayer, I think—
"Lord, bless the dear men who have erected this house
for thy worship; Lord, bless them.   Unborn generations
will bless them when they are gone, and when their toes
are cocking up to the grass roots."   So, in Scarborough,
we find him pleading that the happy time might soon
come when "swords shall be turned into ploughshares,
spears into pruning hooks, and assegais into toasting
forks."

But perhaps one of the most remarkable services of
prayer he ever conducted was in the Hackney Road
Chapel, London, where he took command of the liturgical
service.   Says one :—"It was a marvellous service.
The power and pathos breathed into the old prayers will
never be forgotten. . . . . . .   When he came to
the prayer for the Queen and the Royal Family, he broke
out into extemporaneous supplications for her Gracious
Majesty, full of tenderness and sympathy, that her heart
might be comforted under her great bereavement.   The
congregation was melted to tears."   It was a godly jumble
of the sublime, orderly ritual of the venerable Church,
and the unfettered pleadings of a spiritual nature that
no regulation can confine in any authorised channel, but
it reached the souls of the people, and commanded the
ear of Heaven.

He was so transparently genuine and good that many
of his utterances, which in any other man's lips would
have brought him into the awful clutches of a solemn
Church Court, were passed over with wise, kindly allowance, though not without the shock of a great surprise.
He was the most consistently true man I ever knew.
He could be nothing else, as his family, his colleagues,
his officials, and multitudes of friends can gladly testify.
His charming naturalness drew the people to him, and
made them honour and love him. I think 'I have
intimated that he was a born actor, but he knew
nothing of any clerical stage strut, or mannerisms in
gesture, speech, or tone. He did not cultivate one voice
for the vestry and another for the pulpit. He knew
nothing of the usual commonplaces of so-called religious
expression, and always used English words his varied
congregations knew the meaning of, and could profit by.

It is not for me, or any other, to enter into the
sanctities of his domestic life—alas! he saw little of
these, as his home was so often away from home—
enough to know that his great public pronouncements
on the duties of social and domestic life found beautiful
and charming illustrations in the privacy of his own
house—when the Methodist people allowed him to see
it. That is sufficient. But what about his colleagues?
What have they to say who lived and worked by his
side? It is a very dangerous thing for a man who is
"head and shoulders taller than his brethren" to be
linked at times with small, feeble, suspicious and jealous
comrades. There is a great deal of very human nature
abroad, and the incomplete Church is not without a fair

allowance of it.   Let me say at once that, with perhaps
one exception, at the start of his public career, Mr.
Mackenzie found nothing but loving and discriminating
courtesy and love from his associated brethren.   They
knew his unselfishness and true worth, and often went
out of their way to aid him in many a distressing
dilemma.   And he stood by them.   How he did amuse
me once, when referring to the unintelligent clamour
that was raised in one of his circuits regarding a good,
but somewhat unpopular, brother.   " He's all right, bless
him ; he's only moulting just now," said the man's
cheery apologist and friend.   Yes ; Peter was right.
The good brother in question could never put on the
plumage of a peacock, but has done real service as a
profitable barn-door fowl.

It is more than pleasant to note how ministers so
different in their mental make-up unconsciously join in a
chorus of praise.   Here are a few odds and ends of
brotherly acknowledgment that are surely worth saving
and recording.   No doubt Peter was a somewhat difficult
colleague to handle, consequently the tender, patient,
considerate treatment he received at their hands is all
the more worthy of our appreciative respect.   It was a
good thing for Mackenzie and the Methodist Connexion
that he had wise, generous-minded superintendents to
deal with him.   Let one or two of them say a word here.

One says : " He was grandly happy, and he made
others happy."   Another writes : " Mr. Mackenzie did
not neglect his circuit duty ; arrangements were made
by which he was nearly always present at the anniversary, missionary, and other public meetings in the

circuit, which comprised nine chapels; and his colleagues had the pleasure of speaking to the large audiences that came to hear Peter. We had very little outside help during Peter's term." Said a venerated minister: "You know he was not in my line; but he was a Heaven-sent man, and talked about Divine things in a way that showed he was at home and familiar with them."

Servants, no less than their masters, looked forward to his annual visits with eagerness; and nothing was considered too good for Peter, though his tastes and requirements were of the most simple order. And the children! How he got among them, and stole into their hearts! Mature men and women now lovingly recall how they rode on Peter's knee and joined in his glad merriment. He had a kindly, generous word for everybody, and was almost profusely thankful for even the smallest attention. Yes, he was the miner preacher from the Wear, but the native-born gentleman was apparent in his discriminating bearing to all men. He was a diamond in the rough, but the worth of the stone could not be hid, notwithstanding the absence of the lapidary's art.

CHAPTER XIV.

The Mighty Preacher.

PETER MACKENZIE was pre-eminently a preacher. Although his lectures were unquestionably great, striking, and wonderfully successful efforts, his pulpit work, to my mind, will always take precedence of that of the platform. It was his great first call, and early love; but it is idle now to discuss the overwhelmingly successful attempts to make use of him where financial considerations were all too prominent and pressing. Mr. Mackenzie often told me how he had long battled against this departure from the old order, but the Methodist people would have it, and did, and if there is any blame they must take the "lion's share" of the mistake. Let us recall the preacher. Here are some slight records of his remarkable deliverances, but to those who never heard the man they will sadly need effectiveness. No man can thunder and lighten on paper, and not even a Lucy or Furniss can give a faint pourtrayal of the man. Who can imagine George Whitfield now-a-days, as he stormed from his field pulpit, from his sermons as we read them? It is a matter of wonderment how such productions could have held all kinds of open-air congregations, and to the boundless astonishment and salvation of thousands. "They say," cried a wonderfully gifted preacher, though not over-burdened with modesty, some time since, from his pulpit, "they say men are preaching my sermons. Well, let them; but, let me tell them, they want the MAN!" Just so. Peter Mackenzie may be quoted with more or less correctness, but in retailing the marvellous speaker's words, everything falls short, as no delineator, however honest and graphic, can give us the MAN.

The first sermon I heard from him was in Doncaster, where, with marvellous dramatic action and spiritual force, he dwelt upon the healing of Naaman. After describing the leper, who happened to be a great man— not a great man who happened to be a leper—and who consequently turned away in foolish rage, some faithful adherent spoke up: "Now, master, do get in; Jordan isn't far, and our axle-trees will be well under water; now do." "Turn the horses!" was the loud exclamation of the preacher, and we saw the strange cavalcade wending down to Jordan. There was a halt. The great Syrian was in doubt. "What is the good of this ditch? What about Abana, and Pharpar, and the other rivers of Damascus? What chalybeate properties have these muddy, eddying currents?" The wide-awake servant did not know. "Has any old prophet left any scroll announcing special cures?" shouted the excited preacher. "Don't know," is the only meek response. The great soldier hesitates, but the dramatic preacher cried aloud, "O, I stand by the red river of a Saviour's

blood! Are there any records of salvation on its banks?"
There was an outburst!

> "Millions of transgressors poor
> Have been for Jesus' sake forgiven," &c.

Then Peter imitated the dipping so naturally that
we saw the whole thing. As the preacher disappeared
behind his Bible at each dip the effect was irresistibly
comic, but gloriously realistic. "How do you feel?"
said the servant, as the warrior came up after the
sixth dip. The reply of the shivering man was, "I'm
nearly dead; it's like turpentine!" The quick, earnest
reply was, "Get in, master; only one more," and Peter
disappeared in order to give a surprising bound, with a
loud "Hallelujah!" that fairly brought the whole house
down. I have heard the best interpreters of the great
dead stage masters, but for vivid, graphic realisation of
the fitness of things that sermon in the famous racing
town stands out in the greatest projection that my
memory can command.

Again, when preaching in an old circuit from the
well-worn, but ever-fresh, Psalm, the twenty-third, he
was dwelling on the tenderness of the Great Shepherd.
Early in the service some dear souls could hold in no
longer, and shouted "Hallelujah!" "Hallo," interjected
the preacher, "here are some of the sheep bleating
already!"

A sober-minded Methodist records that he was
astonished to hear the famed expositor say, when
discoursing on the weird case of the demoniac:—"The
Lord knew that bacon was not good for the Jews to eat in
that hot country; but, bless you, it is good for us in

England. A rasher for breakfast, a rasher for dinner, a rasher for supper—you may go on eating bacon, bacon, until you grunt again."

I heard him in Humber Street Chapel, Hull, when dealing with a favourite text, "The Lord God is a Sun and Shield." There was a general outburst of approval among the fishermen and keelmen when he shouted, "One glorious thing about the sun is that nobody can monopolise him. What a blunder they would make. Just you try and focus all his rays upon your own little self. Feel warm and comfortable? Why, man, they would melt you, and there would be nothing left of you but a grease spot."

Thousands of people have heard his quaint, startling reference to the raising of Lazarus. "Why," he asked, "did the Saviour say, '*Lazarus* come forth'? Why did He limit it to Lazarus? Because if He had not restricted it to that one man, such was His power to abolish death, they would have been trooping out of all the graves of the country side."

And it was a great bold flight when he once passionately exclaimed, in referring to the death of Jesus Christ, "When He died, the planet dragged on its heavy course like a great hearse carrying a dead God upon it!"

I give these characteristic fragments without hesitation or apology, since any truthful delineation would be incomplete without them.

A memorable service at Great Ancoats, Manchester, is recorded by Rev. Foster Crozier. Many dear people can only recall the oddities of the gifted preacher, but

let them read and ponder this testimony. "The prayer
meeting then commenced, and, as was his wont, Peter
occupied the lower pulpit, held in an agony of prayer,
his face quivering with agitation, without a dry thread
on him. The chapel, still packed with people, was
veritably a Bochim: groans, tears, sighs, and loud cry-
ings upon God were seen and heard upon every side.
Troops made their way to the Communion, which, though
large, was again and again crowded, so that more than
one hundred persons penitently sought the Lord that
night."

He seemed to know so much about Heaven, whether
pourtrayed under the pleasing and helpful figures of a
country, a city, or the more enthralling symbol—because
the more dearly domestic—figure of a house, or home.
How familiar he seemed to be with the good land!
From his vivid, minute description one would have
thought that he knew every hillside and valley; every
water-brook and fountain; every olive shade and vineyard
nook. And, oh! he knew "the city so holy and clean,"
where every house is a mansion, and every man is a
king and a priest; but he knew the King of the country
Himself most of all.

He found his Master everywhere—in the old Psalms,
the minor prophets, in all sorts of obscure texts and
out-of-the-way nooks and corners of the "Old Book."
Every by-path of his strangely-miscellaneous reading
brought him out on the highway to Christ. He always
knew where he was, and never got lost. Thus he
reached many dizzy heights, to which his daring imagination and true spiritual instincts carried him; but he never

got away from Calvary, and was most at home and effective there. Everything culminated in Christ the Crucified and Christ the Crowned.

Preaching at Wesley Chapel, Bolton, and speaking of the unfitness of an unconverted and unregenerate man for the Kingdom of God, Mackenzie said:—"And every star in the sky will cry 'Away with you!'; and every blade of grass will cry 'Away with you!'; and every sand on the shore will cry 'Away with you!'; and every leaf of the forest will cry 'Away with you!' as you go out into outer darkness." It was an awful moment.

"The most remarkable sermon that I ever heard him preach," writes the Rev. R. Posnett, "was in West Parade Chapel, Wakefield, one Monday afternoon about thirty years ago. It was from the prophecy— 'Behold the man whose name is The Branch; and he shall grow up out of his place, and he shall build the temple of the Lord: even he shall build the temple of the Lord; and he shall bear the glory, and shall sit and rule upon his throne, and he shall be a priest upon his throne; and the counsel of peace shall be between them both.'

"The sermon was thoroughly prepared, and must have cost him very much thought. Every clause of the text was expounded. Once or twice in the course of the sermon he referred to Richard Watson, and he had evidently been studying what Richard Watson had written on that question; but it was in the application of the sermon that the great genius of the man was most manifest. Said he:—'Where are you in

G

this temple—this building? Some of you are stones
in the quarry. Pick and axe have been at work upon
you for many years, and when they failed, God tried
blasting, gunpowder and dynamite. But there you
are still—unmoved, undisturbed; just stones in the
quarry. All the might and omnipotence of God have
seemed in vain. It looks as if, unused and worthless,
you were to remain in the quarry for ever. Where are
you in this building? Some of you are stones got out
of the quarry, chiselled, carved, cut, shaped, but you
have never yet been put into the building. The building
goes up, but you have never got into it. I was talking to
a great builder the other day, and he said it was just like
that with some stones. They come to the works where we
are putting up the building; we carve, and cut, and
chisel them—but, somehow, they never get put in.
They get neglected or forgotten, or they are unsuitable,
so we never find the right place for them, and they
never get into the building; and the result is that
when all the rubbish is carted away at the last, they
go along with the rest of it. You must take care, lest,
by some mismanagement, you are outside the building
at the last. Where are you? Some of you are stones
built into the temple—you have been put into your
place. See that you strengthen the building; see that
you support it; see that you adorn it; see that you do
not fall out of it; see that you help to bring others
into it!'"

Peter Mackenzie is entirely misjudged if he is
regarded as a mere money-making machine. The
minister never forgot his high calling; and his early,

passionate love for soul-winning was never lost sight of.
Peter loved to record big collections—a matter many
"superior" ministers are, I have found, not averse to—but
there are sprinkled through his correspondence brief and
blessed items like these:—"We had a blessed time on
Sabbath—two fine cases, and others feeling."   Again:
"Many seeking Jesus."   And in another note he says:
"Many were seeking the Lord."   Once more: "Two
souls last Sabbath, and thirty-five the Sabbath before,
in my old circuit at Padiham."   Here is another: "Got
a soul last Sabbath"; and yet another—but there are
many more: "We have had about twenty brought in
these last few days at Batley Carr, and some seeking."
Again, he says: "I had six or seven the first Sunday
night."

The man who can joyously record such successes
ought, surely, to be safe from the supercilious criticisms
of some ministers who were too small to measure the
man, and whose ability and success they were utterly
unable to approach.   One young gentleman, with a very
wise look, informed me that he thanked God he had
never heard the man!   He was well got up in approved
clerical attire, but I am sure he lost not a little that
would have, perhaps, brought out what little manhood
was in him.

CHAPTER XV.

PETER MACKENZIE'S lectures were really, after all, expanded sermons, mostly on Scripture characters, and, notwithstanding the unnecessary wail over the stirring evangelist's new departure, I maintain that he preached the Gospel as much from the platform as the pulpit. Could there have been a more solemnly effective appeal than the one in his lecture on "Absalom?" Says the *Methodist Times* in an editorial, "His lectures were full of Gospel truth, and he lit up with a genius all his own the incidents of the Old Testament history, until they lived again in the memories even of the most unimaginative and commonplace of his hearers, while his eccentricities and pleasantries were merely the accompaniments of great intellectual gifts." That witness is true. No minister can be, or ought to be, judged by Draconian laws. No doubt there were at times, chiefly in his earlier ministry, certain things that offended and even shocked the proprieties of proper people, and it may be as well not to let the printer have them. And no doubt he was at

times coarse, vulgar, or rather homely in his references.
Yes, he did take his coat off, when illustrating some
points in his lectures—it is a rare sight to see a cleric
in his shirt sleeves, he looks then so much like other
men—and I have seen him reveal his ample stocking leg.
When dealing with certain characters, no doubt he was
skating on perilously thin ice at times, not a little to the
uneasiness of his hearers. I have no doubt, too, that if
"Mrs. Potiphar" could have heard him, she would have
been anything but pleased; and "Mrs. Jezebel" would
not have felt in any sense complimented; and, perhaps,
on the whole, it would have been better to have left
Solomon's seven hundred wives alone, to fight it out
among themselves. These things were, however, only as
the mote sporting in the sunbeams.

In the making of these marvellous lectures, all kinds
of literary wares were laid under contribution, for which
it is to be feared he got small credit from the crowd.
When engaged on their preparation, he got everything
helpful he could lay his hands upon, and thankfully
accepted kindly suggestions from any quarter. And funny
and merry he was in speaking of those great productions
which delighted and edified the people. In his playful
references to them, he would say of one, just before its
advent: "It's in the egg"; of another: "It's in long
clothes, and will soon be shortened." Another was
"cutting it's teeth"; while one was "having the measles,"
and yet another was "turned out to grass"—fit companion, if it deserved such association, for not a few
venerable sermons whose gaunt outlines reveal the awful
absence of strength and flesh. But Peter dealt in nothing

that was stale or worn-out, and one of his earliest lectures, that on the "Tongue," was more fresh and up to date at the last than it was at the beginning.

When in full swing on the platform he was, indeed, a sight to see. His well-set head; merry, knowing eyes —how much they said!—the indescribable mouth, capable of infinite varieties of expression; and the broad, kindly face—"half an acre of sunshine," as a rough man termed it once in my hearing—lit up by an endless succession of moods only such souls are capable of, afforded a perfect cyclopædia of individuality no limner could hope to put on board or canvas. No snap-shot could get him; and no reporter, however correct and nimble his pencil, could follow the speaker; and the most cunning, practised interviewer must have given him up in despair.

Witty? Humorous? Of course he was—he could be nothing else. It peeped out even in his very prayers, as we have seen. But the wit was clean; no *double entendre* ever soiled his tongue either in public or private, and the children could hear him, and quote him.

Oh, he was no clerical punster or joker—a most pitiable, intolerable nuisance, wherever he turns up. His wit was "mother wit"—his own—and when approaching the perilous ground of sarcasm his lightning was not that of the forked kind, but resembled the sudden, noiseless illumination that plays over the summer hay-fields.

Though he could not claim rank with men whose performances may be described as

    "Faultily faultless, splendidly regular, icily null,"

he was no retailer of other men's commonplaces ; and, in truth, there was nothing commonplace about him. Of course the people laughed often enough at his bright, startling figures and situations, especially when he gave "old world" characters nineteenth-century names, and Methodist surroundings to them. Some who would discount the famous orator can neither make the people laugh nor cry. Peter produced both results, and everywhere. No doubt it was a queer, certainly an "unusual, way of putting things," as Mr. Dawson says, "out of their normal relations to each other and to the world around them." Here are some comic scraps—alas! we have not the great, long, sustained, dazzling flights of brilliancy recorded—which thousands recall with loving appreciation all over the country. Thus, Goliath mistook David at first, and "thought he was a little boy gathering mushrooms." So, when Gideon squeezed the fleece, it was "as dry as the driest sermon that was ever heard." Then again, he gives the ancient Methodist system of finance a sly knock when he says, "A penny a week and a shilling a quarter would have hardly brought grease for Noah's gimlets." Again, "Jacob was not put in the refreshment room, as he charged so much for his porridge," and Aaron was "put off the circuit plan" for insubordination to his superintendent.

Here are some more. If my gentle reader has had enough, he can pass them by. The description of Daniel in the lion's den :—"'Come in,' said Mrs. Lion, placing a chair, 'we don't get a travelling preacher every day'"—a broad hint for the ministerial platform, by the way. And poor Jonah's extraordinary voyage was often

delineated with graphic variations :—"Jonah did not want
to go to Nineveh, so he made tracks. Shortly after
turning into his bunk, the great storm arose and the
affrighted mariners thought it was all owing to the strange
passenger with the long coat tails. Then began the
search, and at length the cry, 'Over with him.' The
passenger rubbed his eyes, and scratched his head, and
asked if they were after his ticket. The captain's reply
was short and to the point, 'Come out, you land-lubber,
you will want no ticket where you are going to'!
Then the great fish took him in custody and said, with
commiseration, as the luckless voyager was hurled over-
board, 'Come in out of the wet,' and the man of so
many strange experiences said, when all came right at
last, 'I was never so sucked in, in my life.' "

My space will not permit me to give names of places
or people, but from faithful lips I have gathered "good
things" that will be remembered for long years to come.
In the North Riding, he was seated at the tea-table in
the vast kitchen of a hospitable farmer, who, in true
Yorkshire fashion, kept open house for the occasion.
The subject of the lecture was "Satan." Several shrewd
questioners asked, in different ways, "What are you
going to make of him?" Peter was silent over his
food, when, all unexpectedly, a great fall of soot—
occasioned, no doubt, by the enlarged fire—swept into
the room, disfiguring not only the table, but some of
the guests. Referring to the question of his friendly
interrogators, he said, with indescribable, quiet drollery,
"He's cooming!"

This forcibly reminds me of an incident at the
Central Station, Manchester. I was bound for London,
and found Peter on the platform of the stirring northern
terminus. He was going to Dr. Parker's City Temple
with his new lecture on the "Prince of Darkness."
Rival porters sought to take charge of his rug and bag
as they recognized him, when the great lecturer said,
in an awfully deep, admonitory tone, "Mind, don't
wake him up; he's inside!" while he stowed his bag
away himself. The good men got their "tip" notwithstanding, and the lecturer got to the Temple with his
strange charge. The congregations at the Temple are,
no doubt, accustomed to wonderful utterances, but that
lecture of the miner preacher left impressions of the
reading, thought, and genius of Peter Mackenzie that
were talked about for many a day. And perhaps for
thoughtfulness and industrious research that was, after
all, the best among his wonderful platform efforts.

Hundreds of wise and witty platform utterances,
more than would fill a portly volume, are treasured up
and rehearsed. Without any connection, I give a few
more. In Mackenzie's own realistic way, he frequently
described the unequal encounter of David and Goliath.
He made his audience *see* the whole thing—the pebbles,
the sling (his own handkerchief, which did all kinds of
miscellaneous duty), and the flight of the missile which
touched the giant in his weakest place, who was "struck
with amazement, as such a thing had never entered his
head before." He would say, in his lecture on Solomon,
"Vanity is the thin end of nothing, sharpened to a
point," and when on John the Baptist, that the intrepid

reformer had "preached to more with his head off than
when on, and without any bronchial inconvenience."
Referring to a case of fatal folly, he spoke of the dead
man as "a candidate for the resurrection." On one
occasion, when rebuking men who imagine the world
will stop when they cease to live, he remarked,
"I will show you how you will be missed. Fill a
bucket with water, then put your hand in it, and
push your arm right in until the water reaches your
elbow : then draw it out, and see what a big hole
there will be in the water. You will be missed as
much as that," he significantly added. On the never-
failing topic of the "Tongue" he was wont to remark,
"Some people's tongues were like an express engine—
a veritable 'Flying Scotchman'—always going at high
speed, with the steam full on; none of your stopping
at twopenny-halfpenny stations, but going ahead like a
western gale." The marriage tie often came in for
illustration, of course, and, speaking of an old Eastern
wedding, he remarked, "The guests sat it out for a week,
and, having neither the *Gazette* nor *Tit-Bits*, it was a
wonder how they got over the time. It seems they had
recourse to puzzles. Well, marriage *is* a puzzle."

Again, he made one of the ten young men who
vowed to erect an altar to Jehovah say to his fellows,
"We had best do it in the night, not only because it
will be cooler, but our enemies are very cantankerous,
very touchy in temper, and very waxy. Ill-natured
people are best to deal with when they are asleep."

When Mackenzie delivered, in the Wesleyan Chapel,
Thornhill Lees, his lecture on Queen Esther—whom he

described as "that rose without a thorn, that diamond without a flaw, that laurel without a seared leaf"—in the course of a quaint amplification of the Biblical narrative, he referred to the sleeplessness from which King Ahasuerus suffered, which caused him on a certain morning to rise very early. After stretching himself and giving vent to a prolonged yawn, he crossed the royal chamber to watch the rising of the sun. In the distance he saw something which aroused his curiosity. "What is yon railway signal sort of thing?" he enquired, whereupon one of the attendants replied, "Your Majesty, it is the gallows which Haman has caused to be made for Mordecai to be hanged thereon." The idea of comparing the gallows to a railway signal—an appliance unknown in those days—caused a hearty outburst of merriment. One of his hearers, now no more, was so carried away with the story, that when Mackenzie, relating how Haman was standing in the court, waiting for admittance, gave a knock, and pointed to the door, he actually jumped up, walked along the aisle, and did not discover how his ears had deceived him until he opened an inner door and found nobody there!

I could give other illustrations of this kind of the famous lecturer's work, but must leave the subject now to the happy remembrances of his friends and the lively imaginations of those who never heard him. I cannot give the MAN.

CHAPTER XVI.

CHARACTERISTIC SERMON.

———

THE parable of "The Prodigal Son" has been handled in every conceivable fashion by sober divines in stately solemn cathedrals, fanes, and by street preachers in noisy or dismal quarters. It is constantly woven into the web of countless evangelical appeals, and is authoritatively quoted in printed matter every day all over the world. The methods of treating it and applying it are endless; but somehow men cannot get away from it. After all the varied expositions, there it stands as fresh to-day appealing to the great heart of wandering humanity, as when the loving words of hope fell from the lips of the Christ ages ago.

Every preacher has a sermon on "The Prodigal Son." Here is an outline of Peter's, for which I am indebted to the *Christian Million*, a spirited, up-to-date paper for the churches, which ought to have a universal circulation.

Full of his favourite theme the excited preacher started off with the exclamation :—

"You will notice that at the commencement of the chapter we read that, 'then drew near unto Him all the

publicans and sinners for to hear Him.' They went once,
and then they felt obliged to go again. Replenished were
His lips with grace, and full of love His tender heart as
they told Him of their simple ways. He told them that
in doing wrong they were sinning against their own
interests and souls. They felt that He loved them. They
went to hear Him, and said, 'I have never heard such
a sermon. It is not like the Scribes and Pharisees. I
have never heard anything like it before.' One publican
after another went to Christ. All characters of sinners
went to hear Him, till at last there was almost a
congregation. But the Scribes and Pharisees murmured
and said, 'This Man

RECEIVETH SINNERS,

and eateth and drinketh with them.' If you had a friend
to have a meal with you in the East, he was as dear
as the wife of your bosom, as precious as the heir,
as dear as the babe in the mother's arms. And they
set down Jesus Christ as a sinner. Christ loves sinners,
and He loves us, but He does not love our sin.
Rather than that we should be bound to our sins, He
gave Himself up that He might break the bonds
and set the prisoners free. It was then that He
consented to give an account of His conduct and His
efforts to save the people. We are not going to find fault
with the Pharisees, for if they had not growled and
complained you would not have had these three parables,
which are the best in the Bible; so that God brings
good out of evil, order out of confusion, beauty out of
deformity. ☉ Christ asked them if it were not a customary
thing, when any valuable property was lost, for there to

be more to-do over it than over that which has not been
in danger at all. 'What man of you, having an hundred
sheep, if he lose one of them, doth not leave the ninety
and nine in the wilderness, and go after that which is
lost, until he find it?' Over mountain and fell and forest,
and amongst wild beasts, he travels and tramps until he
finds the lost one, and then, instead of setting the dogs
at it, instead of complaining about the risks he has run
and the time he has expended, he sets it on his shoulder
and brings it home to his friends and neighbours, saying,
'Rejoice with me; for I have found the sheep that was
lost.' 'I say unto you, that likewise joy shall be in
heaven over

ONE SINNER THAT REPENTETH,

more than over ninety and nine just persons, which need
no repentance.' Whether it refers to angels and martyrs,
Scribes or Pharisees, there is more to-do over the fallen
publican than over ninety and nine of your perfect folk.
Christ gave them that.

"'Either, what woman, having ten pieces of silver, if
she lose one piece, doth not light a candle, and sweep
the house, and seek diligently till she find it?' If you
drop a stud before preaching time or just when you have
to start to catch a train, you will have to get a revelation
straight from Heaven in order to find out where it has
gone. She 'sweeps the house and seeks diligently till
she finds it,' and when she has found it, does she not
call together her neighbours, and say, 'Rejoice with me,
for I have found the piece which I had lost.' 'Likewise,'
then said Christ, 'is there joy in the presence of the
angels of God over one sinner that repenteth.'

"Then we have the

PRINCE OF PARABLES,

the greatest and best of parables, in that of the prodigal son. It is not about a dumb animal or a lost piece of metal, however precious, but about a son who has gone astray from the father. Let me direct your attention to this parable for a few moments. The parable divides itself into three scenes—the son at home, going from home, and returning to home; or we may call them the son's madness, the son's sadness, and the son's gladness. He was mad enough to leave his father's home, sad enough when he had left it, and glad to return to it. He went in for self-government, but didn't he rejoice when he had turned over a new leaf, and got back to the old place?

"May the Lord be with us in speaking and hearing, for His name and mercy's sake.

"Jesus informs us first that a certain man—who represents our Father in Heaven, the Fatherhood of God, the Divine paternity—and there is no doctrine so comforting as the fact that God is our Father. 'Like as a father pitieth his children, so the Lord pitieth them that fear Him.' And when the disciples said, 'Teach us how to pray,' He said, 'Our Father which art in Heaven.' That is the name which brings up sweet and precious memories. When your heart was broken through sin, God sent forth the Spirit of His Son into your heart, whereby you cried, 'Abba, Father.'

'My God is reconciled : His pardoning voice I hear;
He owns me for His child; I can no longer fear.
With confidence I now draw nigh,
And "Father, Abba, Father," cry.'

"He seeks the little children also, and there is no kiss so sweet to the child as the kiss of its father. As soon as God calls, you cry 'Abba, Father,' and you are comforted. He has the Father's heart, the Father's hands, and the Father's provision for you.

"To return to the parable. Christ says, 'A certain man had two sons.' We belong to a very large and ancient, respectable, aristocratic, and noble family. There are angels along with us. There are two branches: an upper and a lower house. We are not going to the House of Lords, but to be heirs apparent along with Jesus Christ Himself. The angels are His servants, and shall keep us in all our ways. In that Heavenly place God Himself is our Father and Jesus Christ our Friend. God has given us a moral straight-edge and a rule, so that we may know how many inches there are in a foot. If we are selling anything, we fancy there are only nine inches to the foot; but if we are buying we say there are fourteen and a half. But God has given us a foot-rule—twelve inches to the foot—and a straight-edge, and says, 'Keep square.' The angels will afterwards come on the wings of the morning and take us home to our rest.

"A certain man had

TWO SONS,

and they were very unlike each other. That is not unusual. I have a family in my mind's eye now. What a good father! What a good mother! What a good sister, and good brother! But there is another one, and he lets them know they are not in glory yet! He *is* a creature! You would not think he belonged to the same family. But such things do happen. If we bring Jacob in and say, 'What countryman is he?' you say, 'I can see by his face that he is a Jew.' Then I bring Esau in, and ask what countryman he is; and you say, 'You have beaten us this time; he is as red as a brick, and as hairy as a worm; he is a cross between a Tartar and a Turk. They are not brothers, but diverse.' So in the same family there is often a great likeness and a great variety.

"Let me direct your attention to the elder brother in the parable for a moment. He is what I call a stay-at-home activity, up with the lark, away with the hounds or pruning-knife all day, and at night in to prayers, and in bed when his father locks up the door. He never broke his father's commandments or gave him a minute's anxiety from the time they rocked him in the cradle till now. Whatever you do, if you have a son like that don't forget to thank him for it; don't take it all as a matter of course. A little bit of praise is always wonderfully cheering and comforting. 1 was told of a mother once who was a slave amongst her family, and worked so hard that she brought herself to an early grave. There was one son, cold-blooded she thought him, who seemed to take everything as if it belonged to him. But when she was taken ill, the tears streamed down his face, and he said, 'Mother, I am sorry you are ill. You have been a comfort to me all my life, and I don't know what I shall do without you.' She opened her eyes a little and said, 'Why didn't you say that before? If you had, I think I should have lived a little longer.'

"But now I want to get to

THE ELDER SON'S BROTHER.

He was a downright forward-movement man. He was determined to do something. He thought that there were three of them messing about the old shop, and that his father had done all the work before his brother was born, so he resolved to clear out. 'They will still have two of them then,' he thought. 'I will take my little bit out, and have a try for it on my own account.' So the younger one, in the hope of getting established in a shop, or a farm, or a place in service, said to his father, 'Please give me the portion that falls to me.' A good deal of property amongst the Jews came down from the grandfather and great-grandfather. Sometimes there would be an injudicious or indolent father, sometimes a father who had a sluggish liver, who could eat well and sleep well, but when it came to work his heart would fail him. So God put into the law a provision that where there was an indolent or spend-thrift father, or one who was good-for-nothing, the son could say to him, 'Give me

THE PORTION THAT FALLS TO ME.'

"So this son said to himself, 'I will get my bit out, and the others may look after themselves.' But he soon found that there were no shops to let, no farms of which he could take possession, and he realised that he must go farther afield. Not many days afterwards he took a journey; and I am not sure that he thought so much as he ought of the aching heads and hearts that he was leaving behind; of her who had soothed his first sighs and stilled his first troubles at

her breast. I turn from all this. I don't read about
the dreadful parting. Poor lad, we must not be too
hard upon him. He had on a new suit and felt quite
a dandy, and as rich as a millionaire. So he took his
journey into a far country, and we will follow him to
his destination and see his conduct there. When he
got to the far country he felt the freedom of a bird
which everyone has a right to shoot at if he has a gun;
as free as the moth that can get its legs and arms
taken off without incurring a doctor's bill, by utilising
a candle; as free as the man going down the rapids
without oars, for he has nothing to do; as the ship in
the Maelström, where she needs no Thames or Gravesend
pilot, for she goes round and round until she finally
goes down altogether. He feels quite free. When he
gets to this country there are landsharks, and, like
detectives spotting a pickpocket, they get their eye on

'VERDANT GREEN, ESQUIRE.'

They know him in a minute, and go up to him and
say, 'Do you want your goods warehoused, or a
respectable hotel, or first-class lodgings, my lord?' He
does not expect such kindness from strangers; and he
invites them to supper, and they are in no hurry to
go. As it is summer time they sit it out, and go home
singing, 'We won't go home till morning.' They were
most assiduous in their attentions, and superlative in
their praises. As they enjoyed themselves so much he
invites them to come again, and he begins to waste his
substance with this living. Never do this. Property
soon goes when there are so many at it; they will

soon run through it. This stupid young man, if he had

BEGUN BUSINESS

with what his father gave him, and made the most of
it, it would have served him through life. How many
are foolish enough to waste their property! Never
do that. I am a Scotsman, and long ago I used to
hear them say that people who worked for ten shillings
a week laid by a shilling each week, and so were above
receiving assistance from the parish. There was a man
out St. Andrew's way, and they told him, 'You need
not be so cocky; we kept your grandfather when he
was on the parish.' Don't be beholden to other people,
but have money in your pocket. 'Waste not, want not.'

"The son soon got through his property, and
when he had spent it there began to be a mighty
famine; when he had exhausted his substance, and his
finances were dried up, and his purse emptied, and his
reputation blasted, and his

LAST SIXPENCE

thrown away, then there arose a mighty famine in that
land! Poor fellow! Of course his friends, if there was
a famine, had to look after themselves; but there are
friends who, if they could, would not help you. Like
the swallows, they make off when the winter comes,
and do not stand to chatter when icicles are about.
'Waste not, want not,' and then God will bless you.

"But you see something good in him after all. I
remember an old Scotchman saying, 'The best place
to pick up a purse is just where you have dropped it.'
This lad said to himself, 'I have been a fool, and spent
my money. I hope to be wise enough to make a bit.'

He did not make up a long petition, and sponge on his father's tenants, or 'buy' butter, eggs, and spring chickens and then sell them for less than the man who owned the hens and cows. He did not start that branch of business; that was left for an educated period. He did not take to the road, and start as a Dick Turpin, or commence to burgle houses, but, like an honest man, he said, 'I will seek for a situation. I am made for work, and here goes.' He

TRIED FOR A PLACE

as steward or ploughman, but there was nothing to be got; he was played out, and there he was, hard up. He thought to himself, 'If I can't screw my circumstances up to my mind, I must screw my mind down to my circumstances: I will take what I can get, even if I have to sweep the streets.' He applied to a man who kept a big house, and asked him if he had a situation for a young man. The man said he was sorry that he could not give him anything, but he sent him into the fields to feed the swine. It showed industry and willingness, didn't it? People then would not let a swine-keeper come into polite society. If a man had 3,000 bogs and 3,000 bright sovereigns, and went to the father of his lady-love and said, 'I love your daughter, and, I think, can make her happy and comfortable, I have 3,000 hogs and 3,000 sovereigns,' the man would say to him, 'Get out, you miserable fellow, or I will set the dogs on you. I would rather marry my daughter to Marwood.'

"There was no one to look after him, and he thought of the time when he was at home, when a servant would stand behind his chair, and many a time he had had a _serviette_, and now he had to look after hogs! The

LIVING WAGE

was not on in those days. The miserable pittance that he got was so small that he could not keep body and soul together. 'He fain would have filled his belly with the husks that the swine did eat.' He never robbed the hogs of a handful of husks. He could starve, but he could not steal. People now squander their own share and yours also, if they can get the chance; but this lad would not steal the husks from the swine. Read your Bible, and you will see it. He could not steal. Husks are poor food too. If you took husks, they would leave your body emaciated and without nourishment, like that of the man who lives on brandy or whiskey or gin. He will not live long, for it leaves his poor emaciated body without nourishment.

"'Then the son came to himself, and there is nothing like

AN EMPTY STOMACH

for bringing a man to himself. A local preacher was once preaching on this parable, and described how the son gradually parted with his garments, first of all his coat, then his linen, then he parted with his singlet, and 'at last he came to himself!' But he came to himself in another sense. He said, 'I will arise and go to my father.' His mind was made up, and he put his resolution into practice. He rose and came to his father. I can't describe to you the mingled feelings of shame and affection that filled the boy when he started home. The father had a presentiment that he would come. He was expecting him and looking for him, and when the son was a great way off, he rose up to meet him. My countryman,

Dr. Guthrie,

used to say, 'I knew a sailor's widow who had only enjoyed the bright, happy time of marriage love for a brief period. She saw her husband go away from the harbour, kissed him a good-bye, and then waited for his coming. When it was time for the ship to return she watched the rocky head and every ship that came into the harbour. She would then go home, and listen to the late passers at night and weep in loneliness. The underwriters gave up the ship, and everyone gave her up for lost, but she still visited the rocky headland and wept and wailed for one who never came back.' But it was different with this one. The father was not disappointed. One morning he said, 'I believe that is he.' He had compassion on him and went out to meet him, and embraced. Matthew Henry says, 'He ran to meet him

WITH THE FEET OF LOVE,

and kissed him with the lips of love.' And the son said unto him, 'Father, I have sinned against Heaven, and in thy sight, and am no more worthy to be called thy son.' But the father said to his servant, 'Bring forth the best robe, and put it on him; and put a ring on his hand, and shoes on his feet; and bring hither the fatted calf, and kill it; and let us eat, and be merry; for this my son was dead, and is alive again; he was lost, and is found. And they began to be merry.' The servants, and the hired servants, the shepherds and the ploughmen

from the plain wefe all enjoying themselves.   Some of
the old servants had often seen the old man with a tear
in his eye; sorrow seeks solitude, but joy courts society.
He could not keep in secrecy then.   He said 'Bring out
the best robe, and kill the fatted calf.'   Instead of the
NASTY, GREASY, PIGGISH
garment in which he had fed the swine, the son now
had on the best robe.   You could smell it four pews off.
Talk of otto of roses and stephanotis, and all the perfumes
of a chemist's shop, it was so fragrant that it would fill
the whole of this church—this best robe.   Instead of
blistered feet, he was dressed in the finest linen, and
there was impressed on him the kiss of reconciliation.
Instead of starvation and longing for food, there was
prepared the fatted calf.   Talk of lamb and green peas!
It isn't in it.   Everyone spoke him a welcome.   All this
is intended to show that the love of our Father is as
high as heaven, and as deep as hell, as immeasurable as
infinity, and as mysterious as God.   He has seen us
afar off and His Son has come all the way from Calvary
to kiss us and bring us back to Him.   The sun that
shines will set; the summer streams will freeze; the
deepest wells run dry, but the love of the Father will be
continuous.   You will require a robe, or you will never
appear at the marriage supper.   Accept the garment, then,
and wear it, and you will be admitted to the feast.   May
you rejoice, and may we rejoice with you in Jesus Christ.
Amen."

CHAPTER XVII.

A Grand Lecture—

"Elijah, The Mighty Man of Mount Gilead."

———

"DEAR Mr. Chairman, and beloved Christian friends,—I, like the chairman of the meeting, am very glad to be with you to-night. You have chosen 'Elijah,' and I hope you will have a good time with him. He was one of the most grand and majestic characters ever presented. Nothing is said about his birth. He comes into the world without a cradle, and leaves it without a coffin. He was made of the same sort of stuff as the heathens made their Gods of—heart of a lion and limbs of steel —and Gilead was the place he came from. When God wants a messenger He doesn't go to some of the schools or seminaries—He goes to the mountains of Gilead, and brings out a man who has graduated in nature's college —one fit for the work. He was fitted for his work owing to three things—by his thoroughness, the force of his character, and, above all, by the grasp of his faith. ? He was

A MAN OF MIGHTY FAITH.

If God said He was going to stop the tap, Elijah knew

He would do it. None of your mumbling, unbelieving sort of chaps—not a bit of it. With regard to his personal appearance, some think he was tall, with long, shaggy locks hanging over his ample shoulders. He had his mantle. With that mantle he smote the waters until they divided, and he went through fifteen feet of water without being wet-shod. His mantle did something more than keep him warm. We see him standing up before King Ahab and saying 'As the Lord God of Israel liveth, before Whom I stand, there shall not be dew nor rain these years, but according to my word.' Our God delights to give us rain. He likes to see all His creatures happy—the little lambs, the sheep, hares, rabbits, and all His human creatures happy, and He has made provision that they should be happy. Why did God stop the rain for three years and six months? There was a reason for it. Jezebel's husband, Ahab, was an apostate from the true faith. He knew there was a God who dwelt on high; but he

APOSTATIZED FROM THE TRUE FAITH,

and he set up, instead of the God of Israel, a worship of Baal—the god of the solids, the god of the liquids, the god of the soul, and the god of the body. With liquids and solids and other things there was very little left for any other god. Jezebel was a true daughter of Baal, and a big bigot. A person who has the least faith is always a bigot—a wretched creature with no more religion than a dog. As a true daughter of Baal, she would keep up the worship. She had four hundred domestic chaplains and four hundred and fifty prophets of Baal. She would make them worship Baal. 'If you

don't worship Baal I'll kill you. I'll cut you up.' Poor
thing! Let a man take to eating too much, to thinking
too much about his stomach, and all his cry is, 'Day
by day we magnify thee.' Let a man do that and he
will suffer for it. The object of the worship will be the
instrument of punishment. Let a man worship money,
and it will starve his body into the grave. Let a
man give way to drink, and he'll get the 'blues,'—he'll
get the 'blues.' Jezebel's Baal worship brought her to
the dogs, and I hope in mercy she was saved. As
Baal was such a mighty god, the Lord Almighty thought
He would let him do a bit of work. He doesn't want
you to be a partner with Him. So the Lord God
Almighty sent His servant to tell them He would

TAKE A HOLIDAY,

and wouldn't do anything for the next three years and
six months. Where Elijah delivered the message is not
known. Some people think he delivered it to Ahab,
surrounded by courtiers, but I think he delivered it
when they were gathered together, as we are gathered
together to-night, when they were praising Baal for
the grand harvest. And didn't they rejoice—the four
hundred and fifty domestic chaplains? And the others
blew the trumpets and the trombones, but they couldn't
blow for ever. They would want nuts and oranges.
And when they stopped for their nuts and oranges,
Elijah gave them a nut to crack which served them for
the next three years and six months. He said, 'As the
Lord God of Israel liveth, before Whom I stand, there
shall not be dew nor rain these years, but according
to my word.' He wouldn't stay after delivering such a

broadside as that; for if he had, when the shock went
off the king would have said, 'Lay hold of that fellow.
What's he come to spoil the meeting for? Lay hold of
him.' But you can't lay hold of a fellow if he isn't
there, and Elijah had absconded. 'And let all the
sinners out of hell, and all the idolators, and all the
Baal worshippers bring a shower of rain out of heaven
during the next three years; let the whole boiling of
them bring a shower if they can.' After Elijah had
delivered that message God came to him, and he had to

CHANGE CIRCUITS.

He was ordered to go to the Brook circuit. 'Get thee
hence, and turn thee eastward, and hide thyself by the
brook Cherith, that is before Jordan.' Many people
would like to make the world without God, to make
man without God, to govern without God, and give
Him an everlasting holiday. How particular some people
are. At the Newcastle conference Primitive Methodists,
Wesleyans, and Baptists were all taken in without being
dipped or baptized; and what is the odds so long as a
man gets put up? And Elijah didn't mind where he
was sent to so long as he was put up. Since I began
to read my Bible I had faith in it, and I have never
shifted my ground, and I won't shift it so long as I
am in this land. They may say I am a dogmatical old
fellow, but I would rather be dogmatical than asthmatical.
When God Almighty says He'll do a thing, I care no
more for the difficulties than an old horse does about
his grandfather. That's about as much as I care for
the difficulties. Some people who hardly believe in
this narrative say, ' " I have commanded the ravens to

feed thee," why the ravens are unclean, and Elijah is a Tishbite, and he wouldn't take anything unclean.' But Elijah wasn't going to

MAKE RAVEN PIE.

The ravens were only the parcels' post; they were the carriers to bring the stuff. You remember David was fed from an ass, and David was particular, and don't you think a raven as clean as an ass any day? The ravens were only the carriers. So dispense your minds about their being unclean. Then, again, people say, 'But ravens don't carry to the nest.' Ravens are very queer birds: they always carry to their nests for six months. It takes them six months to get their family off their hands, and during this period of incubation the male bird brings them something to eat. The male bird sometimes says, in his own way, of course, ' Now, darling, you stretch your wings a bit, and I'll try and keep the youngsters warm, and if you find a bit of something nice, be sure to bring me a bit.' Six months was the exact time Elijah had an appointment in the Brook circuit. Another strong objection is that ravens live on carrion, and, Elijah being so very particular, it was impossible that he would partake of any of the stuff they would bring him. Well, ravens are very aristocratic. They like their food rather gamey. I go to a place once a year, in February or March, on a visit to a gentleman. The game he shoots at Christmas he keeps for me until I go in February or March. Once or twice when I have gone there, I assure you,

THE GAME HAS BEEN VERY GAMEY.

I tasted the stuff when I was two hundred miles from

his place, and when I shut my eyes, although years
have gone by, I can taste it yet. I was once talking
to Mrs. Nicholson, who lives on the hills in Cumberland.
She was telling me about a lot of ducks she had swimming in a pond, and a raven swooped down and took
up a nice young duck from the home of his fathers.
He remonstrated, and the raven said, ' Keep quiet, will
you?' and Mrs. Nicholson never saw that young duck
any more. And who knows but what Elijah was fed
with roast duck minus the green peas? Where would
he get them from? Why, in Ahab's farm-yard. Nothing
pleases God better than to take a rise out of foolish
people. Pharaoh had to educate Moses. He was let
in for all his educational expenses. While the worshippers of Baal were praying to their god, the ravens
were busy picking up the ducks. You must watch as
well as pray. Elijah had beefsteaks—hallelujah!—and
mutton chops and all sorts, ' and the ravens brought
him bread and flesh in the morning, and bread and
flesh in the evening, and he drank of the brook.' I
come now to a period when his time was up in connection with the Brook circuit. The brook began to
run short, because there had been no rain. The ravens
were slow in coming up with their parcels and delivering
their goods, and Elijah's faith would be tried considerably.
And the word of the Lord came unto him, saying, ' Arise,
get thee to Zarephath, which belongeth to Zidon, and
dwell there: behold, I have commanded a widow woman
there to sustain thee.'

' THAT'S PLEASANT,'

said Elijah. ' Why should I always go to a poor circuit,

a place where there is neither a church nor a chapel?
It makes me poorly to think about it.' The stationing
committee always have a good deal of trouble with
the stations, especially with two classes. There is one
class who want a special circuit, and will have them,
and another class who cough, cough with affectation.
I won't say any more about them; they are at the
other end. Elijah made no bones about it, but started
off. When he got there he saw a lonely-looking woman
gathering sticks. So he said to her, 'Fetch me, I pray
thee, a little water in a vessel that I may drink, and
bring me, I pray thee, a morsel of bread in thine hand.'
And she said, 'As the Lord thy God liveth I have not a
cake, but a handful of meal in a barrel, and a little oil
in a cruise, and behold I am gathering two sticks that
I may go in and dress it for me and my son, that we
may eat it and die.' Elijah thought to himself, 'This
is the place for me. It is the right place for the Lord
to work in. He didn't want to send me to a rich old
squire with plenty to eat.' So he told the widow to
make him a cake, and afterwards to make one for
herself and her son. The widow didn't make any bones
about it either, and she made the cakes, and the barrel
of meal was not wasted, neither did the

CRUISE OF OIL FAIL.

She made cakes, and scones, and lots of Yorkshire
pudding—Yorkshire pudding in Palestine! It was a
cake as sweet as Yorkshire batter, and they had it
swimming in butter. It slid down with butter. My
word, she got her cake buttered on both sides of it.
Well, she was a widow, and had one boy, and he kept

very quiet. He fell sick, and one day, when Elijah came back, to his great surprise he found the poor widow sat with her dead child on her lap, and as he came in she said to him, 'What have I to do with thee, O thou man of God? Art thou come unto me to call my sin to remembrance and to slay my son?' She did not know what she was saying, poor thing. Elijah took the dead child, carried him into the best room, laid him upon the bed, and prayed. His prayers became irresistible, and he had faith that God could raise the dead, and God brought back the breath to the body, life from the dead, and the woman knew he was a man of God.

CHAPTER XVIII.

ND the word of the Lord came again to Elijah, and said, 'Go, show thyself unto Ahab, and I will send rain upon the earth.' Everything was dried up; everything barren. The devil is a poor feeder, and Baal was a poor thing when God Almighty withdraws His help. Everybody was CRYING OUT FOR MERCY.

On his way Elijah fell in with Obadiah, who had been commissioned to see if there was anything like moisture at the brook side. When he met Elijah he knew him, and Elijah said unto him, 'Go and tell Ahab, behold Elijah is here.' Obadiah said, 'I feared the Lord from my youth, I had two district meetings to myself. If I go and tell Ahab, while I am away the Holy Ghost will take you nobody knows where to, and when Ahab comes to find you I will be gone, and he'll find me.' Elijah said, 'But I'll show myself to him this day.' 'Oh,' said Obadiah, 'that's a different thing altogether,' so he went and told Ahab, and Ahab said to himself, 'He told us three years ago God wouldn't send rain for

three years, and Baal has been the superintendent of
the circuit. He has been the chairman of the district,
the President of the Conference, and we have never had
a drop of water. Elijah said his God wouldn't send
any rain, and I think our god has gone out of the
water trade altogether. I hope we shall get the tap on
again. That would be sensible, and the devil hasn't
one sensible chap in his possession.' Elijah said, 'What
water has Baal sent you? Hasn't he sent you any?
Let all the people come to Mount Carmel.' There was

A GREAT GATHERING

together inside the hill, which goes about 1,200 feet up,
with the Mediterranean on the other side. In the
pavilion was the king, with his courtiers, the prophets
of Baal—four hundred and fifty of them. Jezebel had
kept her four hundred domestic chaplains at home. It
is supposed they gathered together the night before, and
in the morning Elijah came. When he got near they
said, 'That's him,' and when he got up to them, he
cried out, 'How long halt ye between two opinions?'
He didn't say a word against their apostacy; let them
apostatise. It was their hesitancy. It was their miserable indecision. He did not grumble at their idolatry.
He simply spoke against their hesitancy. 'How long
halt ye between two opinions?' Elijah had a resolution
to put to the meeting, and he said, 'If the Lord be
God, follow Him; but if Baal, then follow him. I,
even I only, remain a prophet of the Lord, but Baal's
prophets are four hundred and fifty. Let them, there-
fore, give us two bullocks, and let them choose one
bullock for themselves. Go and have the first innings

yourselves. Cut the bullock in pieces, and lay it on wood, and don't put any fire under. If your god answers, we'll all join the atheists' society. I'll join you if your god sends fire, but if yours doesn't take any notice, and mine does, serve my God. That's a fair thing. The earth is as dry as a tinder-box, isn't it? Baal's a poor god. He was supposed to confine his influence to the fire and water question. He hasn't done anything in the fire business, and the bottom has gone out of his reservoir. Poor Baal!' And the people went round slowly, crying

'BAAL, BAAL, BAAL!'

And then they warmed up to the work and went faster, 'Baal, Baal, Baal!' But a little before noon they got rather slack, and didn't cry out with so much enthusiasm, and Elijah cried out, 'Are you joining the silent society now? Why don't you speak up? He is a god of aristocrats, and the aristocrats worship him! Perhaps he is talking to somebody. He might have a little cold, and wants his ears syringing. Cry aloud. He is either talking or pursuing. I hope he hasn't been led into some ambush, or has gone on a journey. When did you send a telegram? Did he telephone you? Did he leave his address when he went out? How long is it since you had a post-card from your god? Perhaps he'll never come back, and that will be serious, won't it? Perhaps he went to have a nap. Shout out, and wake him. Shout him up, and tell him we want some fat on the fire.' Elijah said, 'Let all the people come near unto me'; and 'he took twelve stones, according to the number of the tribes of Jacob, and with the stones he built an altar, and he made a trench about the altar as great as would contain two measures of seed, and he put the wood in order, and cut the bullock in pieces, and laid him on the wood, and said, "Fill me sixteen barrels of water."' Sixteen barrels—don't mistake that. The people shouted, and Elijah said, 'Let it be known this day that Thou art God in Israel, and that I am Thy servant, and that I have done all these things at Thy word. Hear me, O Lord, hear me, that this people may know Thou art the Lord God, and that Thou hast turned their heart back again.' And the fire came down in its fullest intensity and consumed the burnt sacrifice, and the wood, and the stones, and the dust, and licked up the water that was in the trench, and when all the people saw it they fell on their faces, and they said

'THE LORD HE IS THE GOD!

the Lord He is the God.' Then Elijah said to Ahab, 'Go home and get some refreshment, because the rain is coming.' Ahab went at once, and Elijah sent his servant seven times to look towards the sea, and the lad came back and said he saw something moist, but perhaps it was only seagulls which had been bathing. Still, he saw a cloud about as big as a man's hand, and he would swear to it. That was quite enough for Elijah. The rain came down, and Elijah girded up his loins and went down before the entrance of Jezreel. And the people said, 'When the king honours the Lord, how the Lord sends rain! Our miserable god couldn't send us any rain for three years and six months. He couldn't send us any fire or water. He reckoned to be a specialist for fire and water, and now he's gone out of both businesses. Your God is a God of fire and water, and a God of salvation.' Ahab went and told Jezebel, but this bad woman was unable to feel the power of good—the horrible creature! She swore by all the gods she would have the blood of Elijah before another sun was set; but Obadiah slipped out some time after and told Elijah he'd better be off, and Elijah went over the hills towards Samaria. He crossed the plains, and did not pull up until he pulled up at Beer-sheba. There he threw himself under a juniper tree, and said, 'Lord, let me die!' But the Lord said,

'YOU'RE NOT GOING TO DIE HERE—

not a bit of it.' He sent an angel, who brought him a cake. He baked it himself, and God gave him a good drink of water, and he let him have it. He said, 'Now lay down. You have only come thirty miles out of the one hundred and eighty, and you have one hundred and fifty to do yet. Lay down and rest a bit.' And he refreshed him twice, and he went on the strength of that food for forty days unto Horeb, the mount of God. When he got there the Word of the Lord said to him, 'What doest thou here, Elijah?' and Elijah said, 'I have been very zealous for the Lord God of Hosts, for the children of Israel have forsaken Thy covenant, thrown down Thine altars, and slain thy prophets with the sword, and I, even I only, am left, and they seek my life to take it away.' 'That's very hard to put up with, I know,' said the Lord, 'but you take too gloomy a view of it. You have left 7,000 members behind you in society who have never cast off faith. You have not

given them their tickets this last quarter. I had a
solitary station once. I put Adam into one once, and
he looked so glum that I put another into the circuit
with him. Mother Eve went to be his helpmeet. I
will send another with you. Go home, and take Elisha
with you.' Well, Elisha was a good lad, and he loved
God. They travelled together for eighty years, and
never fell out. You remember that when Elijah was
going to leave him he told Elisha to tarry whilst he
went to Bethel, but Elisha cried out, 'I will not leave you.
I know you are going from me. As the Lord liveth,
and as thy soul liveth, I will not leave thee.' Elijah
WOULDN'T WANT THE MAN TO BREAK HIS WORD
after that, so he let him go with him. When they got
to the Jordan he took off his mantle and said, ' Ask
what I shall do for thee before I be taken away from
thee,' and Elisha said, ' I pray thee let a double portion
of thy spirit be upon me.' This is true, every bit of it.
We know that Elijah worked twelve miracles, and
Elisha twenty-four, so that he got just a double portion.
'Well,' said Elisha, ' if you are really going, I'll do the
best I can for the circuit.' Elisha took a packet of
salts, and the two stood beside the river Jordan. The
mayor and corporation of Jericho stood a bit off, and
said, ' We have plenty of water, but it is wretched stuff';
and Elisha cured it. He threw in a packet of· salts, and
said, ' Thus said the Lord, I have healed these waters.
There shall not be from thence any more death or
barren land.' When the soldiers came to see Elisha he
did warn them. ' I'll smite their eyes,' he said. ' Shall
I smite them?' said the Lord. ' Yes,' said Elisha,

'smite them with a knife and fork tea. Let them have a good tuck in.' You never saw a Methodist preacher at a tea-meeting look after them as Elisha looked after the Syrian soldiers. When he got them on the road a bit, he said, 'Good-bye; I hope you will find your way. When will you come back to see me again?' 'Never no more,' they said; 'this is quite enough.' Well, as you know, Elijah and Elisha got over the river Jordan, and there

APPEARED A CHARIOT OF FIRE,

and horses of fire, and parted them both asunder, and Elijah went by a whirlwind into heaven. Elisha cried, 'My father, my father, the chariot of Israel and the horsemen thereof, they are off'; and the mantle fell, and the new Jerusalem burst forth in all its glory before Elijah's face. He passed through to the palace of peace. His transmission was sublime, and proves the immortality of the soul. We can't expect to go away like that, but Christ will come Himself for us, and we shall be safe. Let us have His mantle and wrap it right round us; let us have Elijah's faith, and you will pass from this earth into the promised land. May the Lord grant it may be so."

In Loving Memory

OF

THE REV.

PETER MACKENZIE,

THE "GREAT-HEART" OF METHODISM,

BORN AT GLENSHEE,
NOV. 8TH, 1824,

DIED AT DEWSBURY,
NOV. 21ST, 1895.

———

"Who never rested, rests."

———

"Until the day breaks, and the shadows flee away."

———

"Jesus shall reign where'er the sun
Doth his successive journeys run;
His Kingdom stretch from shore to shore,
Till suns shall rise and set no more."

———————

THIS MONUMENT
WAS ERECTED BY A
NUMBER OF MR. MACKENZIE'S
ADMIRERS
THROUGHOUT THE COUNTRY.

CHAPTER XIX.

HAIL! AND FAREWELL!

AT the risk of disappointing many eyes that might be on the look-out for choice bits of the celebrated orator's wit and wisdom, I have thought it best to give in these pages a *whole* sermon and an *entire* lecture, and this course, I trust, will commend itself to the judgment of all who wish to obtain a fair estimate of Peter Mackenzie's public work. Scraps from his lectures and sermons, cut out of their connections, are plentiful enough—perhaps too plentiful, as in many cases they were never his. In a line with a rare order of wonderful speakers of truth, great masters of assemblies, Peter Mackenzie must pay the penalty, like all the rest of them. From brave old Latimer down to this day, the churches have been—yes— blessed with what are sometimes called offensively "humorous" ministers. Here is a constellation: Berridge Robinson of Cambridge, Rowland Hill, Huntington (S.S.), Matthew Wilks, and C. H. Spurgeon. All the churches have had their share in this kind of occasional helpfulness in their ministries; but Methodism has, somehow, discovered and developed—I must not say produced—a wonderful variety of men, eminent in all manner of ways, who have added to her attractiveness and strength. Let us be fair all round. Some good men set themselves to study men and things from one standpoint; another set of equally good men arrange themselves on the opposite side of things; but it is given to some men —perhaps not many—to take stock of life all round. Such men are rare. We are not always invited to a wedding, but it is equally true we are not always called to a funeral. Jesus Christ assisted at both functions, and His followers, whose humanness can hardly be above His, must follow Him. The best and truest teachers and helpers of poor, struggling humanity are *men* who know it in all its conflicting moods and expressions, and *all round*. I have referred elsewhere to famous local preachers, so now here are famous names without whose prominent mention no Methodist history can be complete.

Methodism has had its Sammy Broadbent, Philip Hardcastle, Hodgson Casson, and, in America, its Jacob Gruber, Peter Cartwright, and Lorenzo Dow; and many an unconscious, natural, godly man, who was as terrified at having said a homely, pertinent thing as the charity boy in his school, when he was suddenly pounced upon by the solemn and unexpected vicar with the awfully bewildering conundrum—"My boy, who made the world?" The urchin's stock of knowledge being of the smallest, he could only give answer, "Please, sir, I didn't; if I did, I won't do it again!" The mechanical joker, who acts "Punch" in the pulpit, is out of place, but the man who can, by a mere touch of his unsophistical and unclerical humour, get at the heart of his subject in a moment, is a wonderful help to the crowds which swarm about him.

But I must hasten on. Peter was so good, so generous, so foolish—if you like. At the close of many of his services he would ask for change for gold, in order that he might gratify his noble impulses in ministering to the needs of all sorts of people. Though I go in dreadful fear of my publisher, I must give some illustrated indications of this. Stingy people will not appreciate the subject, but thousands of people will recognise and rejoice in their truthful accuracy. It is only a handful I can give, out of a great granary. These are only mere fragments of the outcome of Peter Mackenzie's unfailing generosity. I have no room to connect them, and they must stand as I recall them.

Railway men of all classes knew him and held him in loving respect. He scattered his silver among them with almost lavish hand. Very few people think of the men driving the mighty engine through the stormy rain of a winter night; not so Peter. It was his invariable custom to salute the driver and his mate at the close of a journey with hearty words of thankful recognition. "You have done grandly; she don't sweat a hair," he would often say, indicating the quiet monster.

The porters everywhere saluted him; a real lord might be stranded, but Peter Mackenzie must be attended to. "How's the missus?" he asked a man hurriedly, as he glided out of a station, leaving a little gift behind him. The woman had been ill for months, and Peter remembered it.

Said a man who had received a double fare, and—
what surprised him more—a kind, generous word, " That's
a rum old party! "   " Yes," I replied; "he is a
Methodist minister."   " Well," said the man, " if they
are turning out that sort of thing now, we could do with
a little more of it down here."

We were travelling together from Leeds for the North
on one occasion, and happened to have in our train a
dozen or more youngsters just let loose from Woodhouse
Grove School for their holidays.   Peter found them out
by their noisy merriment very soon, and on reaching
Thirsk Junction, approached their carriage with his
well-known " Glory! "   There was an answering shout
of approval, as Peter disappeared in the refreshment
room, from which he soon emerged bringing all the pastry
he could lay his hands upon.   Well, the pastry went
before the train did, but the kindly act done to the
children of his brethren will live long in many a minister's
home and in many a boy's heart.

I had the honour of dining with him once at the
house of the late Isaac Marsden, at Doncaster.   We had
a wonderful time of it.   As the dinner progressed, a letter
was put into Peter's hands.   It was from his spiritual
father, the famed Henry Reed, then of Harrogate.   The
letter was accompanied by a cheque for twenty pounds.
Handing the letter to a young minister by his side, he
cried: " Read it again," and, falling down on his knees,
poured out a dozen sentences of thanksgiving, in which
we all joined.   It was the most novel interruption between
the soup and the dessert I have ever seen.   Then the
preacher spent an hour in his bedroom before standing

up in the holy place, and the power of the Holy Spirit was manifest in the public service, and remained for long years to my knowledge.

Hard by there is a village whose affairs were in rather low water. Peter came to the rescue. He travelled from Birmingham to Leeds *via* Doncaster. Of course we had a grand time of it. The dear people were put out of debt and misery by the visit of our friend. "Now, Mr. Mackenzie," said the careful old steward, as he sought to make matters straight with the distinguished visitor, "what shall I pay you?" I seem to see the old man now, with his bony fingers routing in a little canvas bag. "Five shillings is the ticket, Glory!" was the reply.

The dear old saint looked up with brimming eyes and made answer: "Bless God, you shall come again!" I cannot put too much emphasis on this feature of the man's unselfishness. Had he used other, some may say lawful, methods, he might have been a rich man. One who watches the Treasury has the record of His servant, and in many an obscure village the generosity of Peter is remembered as a sweet and beautiful deed.

Mr. W. B. Mason, of Leeds, tells me how—on Peter's arrival at Dewsbury—all the disengaged cabmen would bid for his fare. "Bless you all!" the jaded man would answer, as he stretched out his arms; "I wish I could ride with all of you."

My friend, Mr. B. Halliday, of Leeds, gives me this incident, which reveals the generous bearing of the man to *all*:—"As he went through the different rooms of the mill, he bowed in the most respectful way to the women and girls in their working aprons. 'Good morning, ma'am,' he would say to one and another. In the first room of the mill, where hard, noisy work was going on—the willey room—he was shown a machine, and asked 'What is this chap?' 'The "devil,"' was the accustomed and familiar answer. 'He tears up the wool, and makes it workable,' my friend continued. Peter examined it carefully, and, raising his hands, shouted out, 'Praise the Lord for one devil in the world that is doing a bit of good.'"

I have talked with him about ministerial affairs over and over again, but during a thirty years' intimacy I never heard him speak of a brother minister without words of praise.

On the bright October day when the monument to the memory of Peter Mackenzie was to be unveiled, I joined some working men who, by their manner and speech, were of no accomplished order. "How far is the Dewsbury Cemetery from the station?" I inquired. "Going to a funeral?" said one. No, I was not going to a funeral, I explained; I was going to the grave of a man who had been dead a whole year nearly, and I inquired if they had ever heard of Peter Mackenzie. "He was a rum 'un, and no mistake," remarked a bluff, honest-looking fellow. "Yes, he was all that; but he was a good 'un, you may take your 'affydavy,' and that's more than a common 'davy.'" All the men in the railway carriage had heard the renowned lecturer. Without note of introduction I came in contact with various people whose views I was curious to obtain. On pretence of some small commercial transaction, I asked a tradesman what the stream of well-dressed people, mostly in mourning attire, meant. The reply was, "Oh, it's Peter Mackenzie! I am a churchman myself, you know, but the man seemed to belong to everybody."

No need to ask the way to the cemetery. The hurrying up the hilly streets, and the conversation of the people, evidently bound for a common rallying point, made that evident enough. At a little street corner I addressed myself to two women, who were watching the passers-by. "Where are the people going to?" I asked. Eyeing my note-book, one lady wished to know if I were the "police." Said the other, "They're burying Peter Mackenzie again." I said, "Why, they buried him nearly a year ago!" Said the first woman, "It seems he isn't dead yet, and never will be!"—an emphatic opinion in which her friend joined without hesitation.

Interrogating a carter, who was resting his tired horse on a rather difficult slope, I asked, "Who is this Mackenzie?" The man's contemptuous look of pity I cannot put into words, and, to tell the truth, I did feel ashamed of my ignorance—or hypocrisy. I could only get hold of one cabman, who thought I was in quest of his vehicle. "Did he know Peter Mackenzie?" The man significantly replied, "Well, he'll want no more cabs; and if you get near him you'll be all right." The thing made me a bit uneasy; but I strode up the hill with the unspoken prayer, "Let my last end be like his."

On the hill side, commanding extensive views, I watched the faces, and noted the bearing, of the large

crowd.   It was all Peter—nothing else; but as I saw
the Newcastle express dash by in the valley below, I
could not but recall the tireless traveller, and it was
difficult to realise him sleeping beneath his own Scotch
granite instead of his being miles and miles away,
bracing himself for a great Sabbath effort.

It was well that the beautiful and graceful monument should be placed over the remains of the man of
remarkable gifts, and of still more remarkable graces,
but his memory will be precious with hundreds of
thousands of grateful souls all over England, and whose
reverence and love for Peter Mackenzie will be spoken
of kindly by their children, and children's children.
" His body is buried in peace; but his name liveth for
evermore."

Three thousand people assembled in the beautiful
cemetery at Dewsbury when Miss Mackenzie unveiled
the monument, and revealed the graceful work of the
sculptor set in the firm, enduring granite of his own
north country.   Mr. Dawson gave one more appreciative
address on the worth of his old comrade, and, after
singing the favourite hymn of Peter Mackenzie, the
sympathetic host broke up, and left him near the clump
of trees which the birds will turn into a shrine, and
from which they will sing over him for long summers
to come.

In addition to this memorial—the view of which,
with inscription, is given at the end of previous chapter—
Mr. Lobley has placed a memorial tablet to the memory
of his friend in the Batley Carr Schools.

Farewell, Peter! You will be greatly mourned in the churches, and widely missed by thousands on our cab-stands and "iron roads," by multitudes of men whose only notion of religious life came from your bright, happy exposition of the genuine article.

With tears, I seem to come in touch once more with my old friend, as I mournfully say Good-bye to him.

> "But thou and I have shaken hands,
> Till growing winters lay me low;
> My paths are in the fields below;
> But thine in undiscovered lands."

FINIS.

www.ingramcontent.com/pod-product-compliance
Lightning Source LLC
Chambersburg PA
CBHW021136020726
47500CB00003B/1108